A BEGGAR'S WORTH

A NOVEL

BY EDITH WEBSTER

ISBN: 978-1-63945-034-3 (Paperback)
978-1-63945-080-0 (E-book)

Writers' Branding
1800-608-6550
www.writersbranding.com
orders@writersbranding.com

REVIEWS

I ordered your e-book off Amazon's new offerings and enjoyed it very much. It ended too soon.

— Elizabeth E., Washington

Just finished the little book, 'A Beggar's Worth', and was moved by the characters. I especially liked the mystical slant. Keep writing.

— Ann B., Oregon

I read A Beggar's Worth Tuesday and Wednesday. Small book which still has me thinking. It was an unexpected pleasure.

— Fred B., Oregon

I ordered and read your latest and enjoyed it very much, especially the descriptions of the rags.

— PJ., Arizona

Ordered the new book. A quick, easy, thoughtful read. I have loaned it to my neighbor, who is always looking for authors he hasn't read.

— David T., Arizona

I ordered your book - an e-book, and it was perfect for me for this week. I needed something to brighten up my harsh week. Thank you.

— Dawn H., Oregon

Read "A Beggar's worth and wanted to tell you I loved your descriptions of people and things, especially the beggar's rags.

— Cookie R., Idaho

DEDICATION

This book is dedicated to my daughter Peg who visualized the title. And to friends and family for their encouragement during this difficult year.

CHAPTER 1

The ancient village curved in a natural way around a large bay of murky water. The watching hour rolled in, bringing dense fog inland from the sea as dusk lost all light and the temperature slowly dropped. The lamplighter, back bent against the light wind, mushed into swirling fog as he tugged up his collar and worked his way slowly along the cobblestone lanes. Every night the man started two lanes up the slope from the sea and worked his way down, lighting the way for those still out in the dark.

Lifting his long torch like a wand, the lamplighter touched each oil pot, encouraging a flame to leap before he slowly lowered a globe over each flickering light. As he passed along the narrow lane, small circles of light appeared behind him, vague in the swirling fog as night covered the land at the close of another day.

The lamplighter, no longer young, tugged his collar closer as he continued along the cobblestones, slowly working his way toward home and a warm hearth.

Few in the village were out after the setting of the sun, especially in this wetter season. In the past few weeks, winter became milder, making room for spring, but still each day turned cold after the sunset. Tonight seemed even colder and the fog was as thick as smoke. The increasing wind blowing across the sea inland made the air even colder.

Cobblestone walkways were perpetually damp this time of year but the grouted moss softened the night sounds. The elderly lamplighter took little notice of the cobblestones, moss, or fog as he slowly made his way down the street, around a corner, moving slowly out of sight.

Unnoticed by most passing and unrecognizable as anything of value, a huddle of rags pushed against the rough clapboard wall in an alleyway. The passing of the lamplighter was barely noticed and quickly forgotten by the one huddled there. The young castaway, buried under the filthy mound of rags clutched them ever closer, hoping to ward off the cold wind now sweeping down the alleyway between the buildings.

Working to organize her thoughts, she tried to remember how she came to be here, in this particular village. She remembered being helped by strangers and then later left by someone in a distant village some time back. Not sure how long she waited before a cart heading to this village would let her perch on the back where she was set off, in an unfamiliar hamlet without fanfare, (not sure just yet where *here* is). Or when, must have been near noon, the 12 o'clock hour. Perhaps yesterday or was it the day before? She remembered hearing the noon chimes when she first arrived.

Yesterday, she thought. Confusion seemed to fill her days lately. The long winter had taken too much from her. She wondered now if she had the will to survive another cold night. Her imaginings, both through long nights and bleak days of lack, kept her from giving up but perhaps it had all been a futile exercise from the very beginning. She tried to think, to remember when her dreams of a rich wonderful life became a mirage, carried away on the cold relentless wind. She almost laughed as she remembered her grand plan in the beginning and all the dreams never realized since.

She moved her outer rag covering and looked toward the vague circle of light beneath the tall standard at the end of the alley. Without understanding why, she began to make tiny, miniscule shifts toward the light. Slowly but surely the pile of refuse eased into the light and settled close to the lamppost. She felt a small measure of pride in reaching her goal before succumbing to weakness. Someone passing gave her a drink of water, but that must have been hours ago. Her thoughts were jumbled.

The perception that light brings warmth is not always a true perception. In this case it was not, but who is to say what each creature imagines. She felt warmer.

As the mound of foul smelling rumble moved into the circle of light and settled next to the tall, scrolled iron fixture, her movement stopped, but not before a small filthy claw-like hand, crusted and soiled, reached through the layers to pull a piece of treasured refuse closer around herself.

Her cracked lips tried to smile. She hoped in some hopeless way for a bit more warmth, remembering from some distant time the image of a candle, or possibly a warm hearth. A kettle hanging full of hot broth. Those would be later memories. There were no early memories of warmth in the shack of her birth.

The fog thickened as the moonless night closed in on the coastline and hamlet. All became inky-blackness except for the row of oil lamps flickering down the cobblestone lane.

The temperature continued to drop; the cold breeze turned slowly into bracing gusts of wind as the clock in the tower struck midnight. The huddled pile of refuse drew even further into itself, becoming smaller. A truer picture of utter misery would be most difficult to imagine. The long night hours drug on.

Unbidden memories surfaced, coming in unwanted waves.

The home with a cold hearth, the lack of food, a mother worn down by daily cares. The life of a peasant held little if any hope, truly a place to run from. So, she ran. Her longing to find freedom out in the vast, unfamiliar world became a force not to be denied. There were glimpses of riches to be had if one could find the path. They were there to be taken. She was sure of it.

In the end, it all became a cruel deception. Life became a tangle of dissolution and loss through the months that followed her grand exit from her life of poverty. Only to end here, near death, cold and alone.

With no tears left to cry she shook her head and fought to remember. She knew she must have a name. In fact, she used several in months past but her name, the one her mother gave her - think! Sophie! that's it. Sophie Something.

A soft smile came, for a moment celebrating. Sophie, just Sophie Something. That would do for now. She used several names at different times, so her surname became lost in the confusion.

CHAPTER 2

Numb from exhaustion and unsure, Sophie thought she felt something shift in the space around her when her mound of protection absorbed a minute tremble. Lifting her head an inch or two, she waited. Was it an ever so slight 'something' different or just a stronger gust of wind pushing in from a different direction? The pile of rags re-settled. She grew still, trying to find a measure of comfort, wanting to sleep, perhaps even be fortunate enough to die. She remained aware on some level of the increasing dampness and pulled her rags closer. And the possible dangers just beyond the circle of light were never far from her mind.

The earth moved again. The feeling of possible danger came, along with fear, and questions. What could it be? Now and again the bell of a ship in the harbor could be heard off in the distance, but one didn't feel ship movements in the bay, or did they? The good citizens of the city were no doubt bolted in their homes, snug in their beds at such an hour on this inclement night, sleeping undisturbed.

No alarms could be heard sounding in the distance. Sophie understood there were no folks near, no one to call out to. Not at so late an hour. She felt a new and unexpected level of terror.

A few moments later she felt the trembling of stones, followed by a muted sound, still distant to be sure. Not a port sound, not the usual sound of an ordinary trap passing by. No, whatever approached bearing forth with weight and such speed was not the ordinary-every-night sound. The earth shook, the sound grew louder. It must be something massive and moving at such a speed to force the cobblestones to crush around her. The clamor grew ever more intense as the shaking of the ground increased. Some kind of conveyance *was* coming, drawing ever closer. Sophie moved - still mere inches from the iron post, unsure. The light of the lamp, though barely discernible in the mist, gave a false feeling of protection. The thought came but quickly went to try to regain the protection of the alleyway, but no strength remained to make such a move. She knew she could not move, weak and trapped in fear she could barely breathe.

In the end, the heap of rags barely shifted, simply not enough strength to shift even an inch further much less the distance to reach safety, somewhere outside of her circle of light.

In what seemed like a moment, no longer than the blink of an eye, the new different sounds approaching could be heard, sounds began to separate. Hooves clicking on stone, wheels rattling across the uneven terrain. A whip now and again cracking, the driver encouraging beasts onward; her eyes wide open but still nothing visible.

With unexpected suddenness, the fog separated and a huge, ornate coach drawn by six beautiful perfectly matched animals came into view. The driver, whip in hand, was dressed warmly and well. His attire so colorful, gold buttons flashed, even in the limited pale lamplight from one lamppost to the next. Tops of two footmen's heads could be seen riding the rear of the magnificent phaeton. Sophie felt her breath catch and hold.

CHAPTER 3

The destitute soul peered out through an opening in her collection of rags and was mesmerized watching the approach of the mystical vehicle, knowing it would be away, out of sight soon. Her mind filled with the vision of such power and beauty, knowing it would be gone as quickly as it came. Traveling at such speed it would be nothing more than a vivid memory in a few short moments.

Moving at an incredible speed, the vision was now practically on top of the post with her and her pile of rubble pressed against its base. The whole of the vision including the horses were floating above the ground but still with noise all around. All of it so unreal, so impossible, but so beautiful…

At the point of passing, a voice, clearly heard but not shouting, gave a command. "Stop the coach."

"Whoa, whoa there, easy now!" The elegantly dressed driver and the two footmen heard the command and instantly performed in a perfunctory way to obey, no easy thing considering the size and weight of the coach, not to mention the speed at which it was traveling. Six strong matching horses some distance above the ground pulling in tandem was a force to be reckoned with. Nevertheless, the horses and large floating carriage settled to the cobblestones and was completely still in what could not have been more than a few seconds and was now not more than three or four lengths from the lamppost, *her lamppost.*

"See the bundle? Bring her to me. There is a chill, be quick now." The voice full of authority, yet gentle.

"What bundle, Sir? There is nothing to be seen but a pile of refuse by yonder light." The two footmen, anxious to do as their master instructed, seemed at a bit of a loss. They could see nothing but the heap of trash in the pale circle of light, still they waited for further direction.

"There beside the column. Bring the bundle to me. Be gentle" The two footmen moved quickly to obey, careful to pick up the foul-smelling mound of rubbish, leaving nothing behind. Reaching the coach, one footman opened the door, the other one stepped inside, settling Sophie and her possessions on the seat opposite the only other person in the coach.

"Well done." The gentleman nodded, "Best get home now, out of this foul night air." The warmly dressed man inside the coach looked at the bundle now seated across from him and then turning, glanced toward the footman. The footman jumped quickly down from the coach step. "Aye sir, home it is." while shutting the door of the coach firmly with a snap. In mere seconds the coach once again sped ahead through the dank night.

CHAPTER 4

The mound moved. Sophie's thin hand pushed the last bit of wool cloth off, revealing her face. The older, well-dressed gentleman seated across could clearly see her face now, her eyes wild with fear and confusion.

Sophie tried to breathe as she looked at the richly robed gentleman seated on the plush bench opposite her. He looked to be a large man, perhaps taller than most, with a head full of white hair and kind eyes. Neither spoke. The coach sped on.

As the warmth inside the coach soaked through the damp rags protecting the young lost soul, she felt the cold vanish and gave in to physical weakness. Unable to keep her eyes open she slipped into oblivion. Though fear still tried to ravage, she quit fighting, permitting sleep to overcome all else. Blessed sleep that pushed off fear, hunger, pain and so many memories of life's abuses, (both earned and unearned), so many mistakes: she fell into a troubled sleep. Slender bands of steel began to release deep inside and a gentle rest slipped in.

She did not want to remember – there had been times the stabs from the past seemed so deep she would bleed. Though weak and exhausted some memories sifted up unbidden in her dreams.

Yes, months ago a moment in time opened and she had run from the only home she knew, nothing more than relentless poverty. Too many mouths to feed, never enough food to push hunger off for any length of time.

Her first few weeks of her newly found freedom and short-term goals of changing her world for the better unfolded well. She reached the city and found a position as a lady's maid to the daughter of a Nobleman. The fat uncouth fellow with half-lidded eyes also lived in the home with his daughter. Sophie stayed clear of the master as much as possible and there were many things to enjoy in the new position but being dismissed for stealing with no letter of recommendation made positions, afterwards more difficult to secure.

She did not steal. Truly, she did not. It was all a terrible misunderstanding. Her mistress was away for the afternoon and Sophie saw no harm in trying on a gown of silk and trying some of the many sparkling jewels to complete the overall effect. Seeing her reflection, seeing what a difference these changes made caused her to almost miss the sound of the return of her mistress.

Sophie hurriedly removed the gown and most of the jewelry. She was trying to remove the last ring when her mistress entered the room. Unable to explain and, with words of apology stuck solidly in her throat, she was summarily dismissed.

From that respectable station and without a letter to recommend her, she was finally able to secure a scullery maid position that lasted several months. The work was heavy and hard with long hours, usually finishing late into the night. The place to sleep and the food provided was filling but there was nothing else to commend the position.

Sophie left that post of her own accord and was not sorry to leave when she was offered a position as under-attendant wardrobe mistress to a troupe of traveling players. Traveling about the countryside, seeing a new and different part of the world each week renewed her dream. The dream of becoming Nobility. She understood one's station in life was set on the day of their birth but the dream of riches could not be quenched.

Nothing lasts, change will come, and alas, although the shabby troupe of players brought joy in the beginning, she found several of them to be disagreeable people. After only a few summer months, she admitted that she hated the constant conflict between the players. When they were off stage some of the actors were especially vile towards the other players. Sophie was mostly ignored and preferred it that way. She grew to despise the constant cold insults hurled at each other. Once they were on stage, they all put forth a jolly front, pleasing the crowds but, in the end, the poor food and false behavior of most of the players in the troupe left her more than ready to strike out on her own in search of a well deserved new and better life.

Nothing went as planned. One wrong turn after another the following months brought her to the final degradation at the base of the lamppost. Without knowing how, without understanding why, her dreams became just that, vague dreams full of misery.

CHAPTER 5

Startled awake by the lack of motion, Sophie did not move. She waited, uncertain what to expect next. The coach now stood at rest. In the moments that followed she both heard and felt the footmen jump down and almost instantly open the door of the coach. She looked first at the door then, with eyes still filled with sleep, she turned to look at the man seated across from her. Tipping her head up slightly, her gaze pulled against her will, she looked into the eyes of the figure seated there. Her emotions changed from fear to puzzled wonder as she felt the unexpected shift ricochet through her, all terror receding. Dressed plainly and yet somehow clothed in elegance, the gentleman made a slight nod but did not speak.

Something about him caused Sophie to be overwhelmed with her insignificance. Certainly, an emotion she'd felt before but never to this degree. She shrank back. She could have laughed at the thoughts now filling her mind. The strange man with the kind demeanor seemed to her much like a St. Nicholas mentioned by others. An older gentleman with heavy white hair who brings gifts to nice people. The imaginary Nicholas had never brought anything for her but she'd heard stories of such in her treks from place to place.

She glanced again at the person across from her, with her head and face still mostly covered. The man sat folded into the soft cushion's, eyes closed. Sophie heard the soft clang of the steps of the coach being lowered. The gentleman seated across from her shifted and prepared to rise. Sophie felt a warning course through her. She knew she could not trust her impression. The eyes held kindness, a gentle strength, and beyond that an authority. But she would not let herself trust what she knew would soon be revealed to be false, possibly even cruel. One gradually learns to trust no one. This became her mantra for many months and helped her to survive imminent danger more than once.

The well-dressed gentleman stepped down from the coach onto the cobblestones that formed a circle drive in what must be his home. His boots shone from the light of torches along the walkway leading to the steps up to the portico of a huge building. Large doors formed the entrance to a stone structure so large Sophie thought of castles she had heard of and wondered if this could be real.

Sophie watched the gentleman with the full head of white hair climbing steps and being greeted by people before noticing the footman, now leaning into the coach. "Come. You are quite safe now."

Sophie, still thoroughly warmed from the coach ride, felt too weak to move. She could only stare at the outstretched arms. The footman wrapped his strong arms around her and gently lifted her with all of her possessions out of the magical coach and carried her up the steps and through the huge door into the castle, where he carefully settled her. Sinking to the floor, Sophie remained motionless in her nest of belongings with only her eyes uncovered. The entrance was large with shiny floors and many lit candles. She wanted to stand but her legs would not bear her weight.

A young man approached from a side doorway into the hall. "I heard the coach and came to see if you needed me." The king-like figure spoke, "Thank you, Henri. Go call Mary Elizabeth and ask her to come. I believe she is the one we need now and she may need for you to stay and help."

The tall, thin young man nodded his understanding as his eyes met those of the Nobleman. He then turned and quickly started up a wide curved staircase. Sophie caught the exchange between the two before noticing others now gathered in the large clean space around her. The man with the mass of snow white hair from the magic carriage that floated on air was greeted as a king by those coming near. They all looked warm, well dressed, well fed. Even happy.

Sophie knew she would feel the harsh truth soon enough. For now, she would press down her emotions, try to stay calm. Strange weakness and total confusion threatened. Looking down she touched the rags around her. Her things. They looked the same as yesterday except she knew she was weaker from lack of both drink and food. No longer cold, she tried to curl and uncurl her fingers. Peeking out again she wondered, *'Who are all these people?'*

Things became less clear. She closed her eyes, once again feeling defeated and alone, desolate. Shame crept in from nowhere. She let her chin fall to her chest and waited for whatever should come next.

Before when in desperate straits, she would just wait. That seemed the best defense now. Wait for an opening, perhaps when she regained strength. She would find a way in time to escape. Just keep her wits and watch for an opening. She knew it wasn't much of a plan, but it would have to do for now.

CHAPTER 6

Sophie lifted her face and tilted her head to the side to peek out of her covering. A soft rustle could be heard. Sophie noticed heads turning. Those around her were all looking in the same direction. She lowered the scrap covering her eyes a bit lower hoping to see better. She finally pulled the piece away from her face.

The curved stairs were to Sophie's left. At first, she could see only the near steps, then a slipper followed by the hem of a garment became visible as she lifted her gaze. A garment so beautiful worn by a woman who seemed to float down the stairs toward her, a slender hand sliding along the banister.

Envy filled Sophie's throat like a gorge, thinking, "*anyone could appear beautiful when lavished with wealth so apparent as seen here.*" Thick auburn hair, pulled back from a face without blemish and big brown eyes filled with warmth, lashes long enough to lay on cheeks when blinked. Perfect lips shaped in a perfect soft smile. Sophie thought '*she is too beautiful to be real. Where am I?*'

The beautiful person stepped near the man who must be the king of the castle and smiled. As she straightened from a curtsy, her eyes shifted for mere seconds to where Sophie remained mostly covered in her belongings.

Sophie watched, mesmerized as the woman spoke, "Ah, dear Abba, you have been out and about again I see. May I take care of this new little one for you?"

Soft words full of authority fell on Sophie's ears. She heard him say, "Yes. Please call Monika to help. And Henri, of course." When he finished speaking, the man turned and left the vast entryway through a side entrance. Sophie heard someone say, "Here comes Monika." The one called Monika skipped into the foray, (she skipped as naturally as an eagle flies). Sophie felt a smile trying to force her lips to move at the sight of the small bouncy human. Her straight brown shoulder length hair with bangs straight across her forehead continued bouncing as she moved toward the beautiful tall woman.

Monika covered her nose and stuck the tip of her tongue out of the corner of her mouth as she bent to give a slight tug to one of Sophie's treasures. The small woman smiled her whimsical smile up at Mary Elizabeth, who stood at least a head taller than this small sprite of a woman. Sophie assumed she must be some kind of assistant to the lady called Mary. To assist in what way was a mystery.

Mary returned the smile with one of her own and a nod, "We will be busy for a bit I should think." Sophie heard the same tone of authority with gentle warmth, from the beautiful woman as first heard from the one called Abba.

The tall slender man first seen and heard by Sophie when she was carried into the castle, returned and stood quietly on the scene. He stood waiting for a nod from Mary. The beautiful woman looked down at Sophie and her belongings before giving instruction to the tall one called Henri.

Henri lifted Sophie and the filth wrapped around her and carried her as directed by Mary toward a narrow passage just as another small woman came into the huge hallway, saying, "Darla is again suffering melancholy so it will be me and you for today." Monika nodded and smiled, "Oh, the two of us should do, Bridget. We will be all the help Mary needs, I should think. Thank you for coming." Tipping her head down, Monika became thoughtful for a moment, "Yes, the two of us should be enough, I think, and Mary says we are a good team!"

Monika let a small frown cross her brow, "We will check on Darla later. I just wish we knew how to help her." A soft caring expression crossed between the two friends, Bridget and Monika, before they began to list off all they would need for the task now before them as they followed Mary from the castle entry.

"Let's go see where Henri has put our newest guest, shall we?" Mary started down a narrow hallway. "Abba would be very displeased if we lost one after he went to the trouble of finding her." Sophie heard the chuckle.

"We are yours to command! You lead and we will follow." The three women laughed, mostly because of the way Monika spoke. One could always find a trace of humor in the women's conversation even when facing difficult work. They knew the task before them this night would not be an easy one.

The women entered a small bathing area. Henri arrived just ahead of them, and while still holding Sophie and all her belongings in his arms, looked at Mary for further direction. Mary touched his arm, pointing toward a padded bench, "Leave her there until things are ready. Be gentle, settle her with care."

The one called Henri settled Sophie on the bench, careful to gather her possessions around her.

Sophie longed to just let go, pretend she was far away in a different world. She used to do that when there were books with wonderful stories but there were no books here today. The hour was late and she had slept in the coach but still, she felt overcome with weariness.

The two small ladies, Monika and Bridget, put their heads together. Thinking only of the task ahead, they became serious. Mary Elizabeth was in charge of course, but still the two friends whispered, "Could be this one will need special care."

Monika glanced at the sad creature on the bench. Through the small opening in her rags, Sophie could see their faces and thought about shouting at them or maybe spitting at them. Maybe she could just fall off their bench in a heap and give them a bit of a fright! They whispered their stupid chatter as though she couldn't hear them. She pulled a scrap slowly closer and did nothing, simply no remaining strength left to fight, or for that matter to care.

Sophie remained still in the middle of the activity around her and began to study the three women. They all appeared so different; one tall, beautiful, with large brown eyes and so much dark auburn hair pulled back and wrapped in some kind of ribbon. This one called Mary moved with a grace Sophie could only envy. Everything about the women seemed perfect.

The one called Bridget was the smallest of the three with long, fine soft blond hair and blue eyes. Her hair, held by a ribbon, was pulled back and to the side, falling over her right shoulder and down in front. She was the shortest of the three. and appeared more serious in nature than the other two. All three women were dressed in beautiful gowns. This puzzled Sophia since the hour was late. As Sophie watched, all three donned long white aprons, preparing to do what?

CHAPTER 7

The three women became very busy with all kinds of preparations - laying out assorted things, some familiar to Sophie, some not. The one called Mary instructed the two attendants to use the longer list of things needed for this new one tonight. The beautiful lady looked directly at Sophie and said, "We will need the healing ointment this time, too." Monika heard and understood. Sophie heard and wondered.

Monika and Bridget tied and checked each other's aprons, still whispering. Now and then a chuckle could be heard. Sophie felt a softening deep inside. Though still uncertain and shaken, she could not remember such gentle patter between women. So much of this night felt magical, at least since the mystical coach found her.

Mary turned, surveyed the room and touched a finger to her chin, "We will need a basket for discards, a large one I think for things no longer needed." Thinking aloud, she said, "And a burn container."

Sophie heard but did not understand. She flinched. Mary noticed the flash of pained expression, before speaking softly, "Monika and Bridget can be trusted. They will do you no harm. I love and trust them both and hope you will grow to love them in time, too."

Waiting now with armloads of things needed, the two small women waited and Bridget said, "We are ready, Mary Elizabeth. Should we call for the water?"

"Yes, find Henri and ask him to get as much help as he needs. We will need many buckets, and as hot as they can safely carry." Mary kept her voice soft and low.

"Will do. I will ask for plenty of help so the water will be steaming." Bridget turned to leave with Monika following.

The two small women looked at each other and chuckled, "We like a bit of hard work but not helping with the water." A pause, and chuckle before Bridget said, "We are too short!"

Returning from instructing Henri, the two small friends rejoined Mary. They stepped closer to Sophie and her possessions. They understood the challenge before them. Sophie could only guess. While they waited for Henri and the others to bring the water, Mary sent Bridget for a cup of hot soup and a pitcher of cool water. Monika trotted along with her friend to fulfill the request. When they returned Mary, brushing back an errant strand of hair said, "I think the three of us will do just fine. As the men carried in steaming buckets of water, Mary handed Sophie a cool drink first, followed by the hot broth.

Sophie feared she would be sick when the broth began to warm her. She wondered at the thought of feeling embarrassed, she'd been sick many times before without feeling shame. This felt different but she need not have worried. The cup of water was cool and satisfying and the hot broth brought strength to her weakened body.

As a measure of strength returned, Sophie glanced carefully around the room. She felt the old paralyzing panic, no avenue of escape could be seen.

Sophie's fears overwhelmed her for a moment, before being whisked away by the gentle sound of Mary Elizabeth's laughter. Placing a lower stool close to the full tub of steaming water, Mary helped the girl shift from the bench where Henri placed her earlier to a different stool by the tub of hot water.

Suddenly something new came reeling through the girl's senses: an incredible fragrance filled the room. Sophie closed her eyes and knew she'd never encountered anything so wonderful. Nothing in her short life could compare.

Sophie felt a hand touch her, "Please drink a little more water." Mary held the goblet with both hands as Sophie drank the cool water.

"Now drink a bit more of the broth. Please. It will restore some much needed strength to you." The voice of the beautiful lady wrapped around Sophie as a command that did not feel like a command. Sophie sipped. Uhm, it felt tasty and warm on her tongue. She looked up into the beautiful face, seeing an expression as warm as the broth. Sophie said, "Thank you." as a small measure of strength spread through her body.

Mary stepped back and waited, letting the girl hold the cup. Sophie handed her the empty cup, hoping her belly didn't rebel from the broth. She no longer seemed capable of controlling what her body would or would not accept. With a deep breath, she hoped for calm. Strength filtered into the fibers of her being, thoughts became clear. Memories of when she last tasted something good could not be found. Other memories did sweep in - pieces of the past began to float up from a lake of misery.

As her strength renewed so did her wariness. What could these strangers want from her? She owned nothing of value, nothing. That surely must be obvious.

Sophie breathed a shallow breath, waiting. No need to be anxious, whatever their plan, it would be revealed in its own time. No need to resist. If the past was any kind of teacher resistance rarely offered any kind of advantage. Something she learned, mostly through trial and error. The broth and freshwater were worth whatever the cost. So far there was no charge mentioned.

Sophie watched the three ladies set about preparing. Preparations involving her no doubt. Again, Sophie caught a heartful of the fragrance, so rare it brought an unfamiliar ache.

The little lady called Monika laughed, "Abba sure has a knack for finding things for us to do."

Mary Elizabeth smiled, "I think it is his way of blessing us. Helping us to grow, be more worthy tomorrow than we are today. We think we are doing what needs to be done and we are. But the reward that comes is another building block in us." she paused, catching Monika's raised eyebrow and quirky expression, "We need all the help we can get; don't you agree?" Her soft chuckle followed. Monika and Bridget both snickered, knowing they would do all they could for this person now bundled before them, so in need of all they could give. And a '*well done*' from Mary when finished held a reward to be prized.

In the past, Mary, on more than one occasion, expressed her pleasure in working with and spending time with Monika and Bridget. Both women, small in stature but huge in willingness to do the hard, unpleasant work of polishing a lump of clay in search of the diamond hidden inside, seemed to relish what others often shunned. They filled with excitement with each new arrival needing their help.

Some of Abba's finds took a great deal more work than others, but these three seemed to embrace the challenge.

"Thank you for the larger basket. As we work, I will make a judgement of each piece. But I think most, if not all, will no longer be needed." Glancing at the large basket held by the two attendants, Mary said, "That should do." The women stood ready, knowing this part of the process could be difficult.

Mary smiled and nodded at her two friends, letting them know all was now ready, time to begin.

CHAPTER 8

Rolling up her sleeves, Monika said, "Well, what are we waiting for? Let's get about it while the water is still hot." The room now overflowed with fragrant steam.

Mary, now on her knees, glanced once at Bridget to make sure she held the rubbish container near enough to reach. She then rested her gaze on Sophie, "Please try to remain calm. Truly, we are here to help you. We are going to disrobe you now."

Sophie's mind screamed, *"Disrobe me, take my treasures, my protection, each piece hard fought for! No no no!* Clenching her jaw, she stared straight ahead, made no sound. Mary noticed but let the moment pass.

The first piece of Sophie's possessions Mary lifted off was the old substantial scrap of wool, what remained of a once large blanket. Aware of the pain she caused by removing it, Mary gave Sophie a moment to clutch the possession close to her chest one last time before pulling it away and handing it to her two helpers for disposal. Sophie was grateful, she needed that moment to let go. The filthy piece of wool kept her warm on past cold nights. She watched Mary hand the wool to Monika saying, "She has felt protected by this possession, both from the cold as well as from many hurts, especially rejection. Rejection brings along with its loneliness, heart-felt pain, and so much fear."

Sophie's eyes opened wide, looking at Mary with both wonder and apprehension.

Watching her reaction, Bridget looked at Monika with a small smile, Monika winked at Sophie, saying, "Mary Elizabeth is gifted with knowing things at times." Pausing, she continued, "We are used to it. Do not be afraid."

Mary closed her eyes, her brow creased. Was she feeling some kind of pain of her own? Sophie watched and marveled at the way the crease slowly smoothed across the woman's brow.

"If you can, I encourage you to release all the feelings of rejection and the various fears attached that have been stored away for so long. Some may even feel a bit like old friends but they are not. Our hope is that, in time, you will be able to trade all fear and rejection for acceptance."

Looking directly into Sophie's eyes, Mary said, "Truly, here in Abba's home you will be accepted. What you do with that acceptance, of course, is up to you. Every evil, spoken of here today also has many facets of positive good. You will learn ways to overcome all of your fears and replace them with things like joy and peace if you are willing.

Sophie felt a tremble roll through her body. A real place for her, a home! In a castle! Was such a thing possible? For just a moment she felt a desire, a need to believe before emptiness filled her once again. A new kind of terror filled Sophie's eyes as she lifted her face to look at the one called Mary. She was the one to watch. Obviously in charge of the others. Yes, she would be the one to watch!

Mary spoke aloud to her two assistants, all the while looking directly into Sophie's eyes. "Even in the darkest places in the universe there is good news. For every negative and evil thing on earth, there is a positive opposite. For example, rejection can be and is replaced by acceptance."

Mary revealed a slight smile as she continued, "If one is willing every negative in their life can be changed over time. All things can become positive. Positive in every area of one's existence."

The two willing assistants watched Sophie, understanding how Mary taught without really thinking of it as teaching. They stood ready now to receive the next piece that would be discarded, both nodded their understanding as they waited.

Sophie began to feel sick. She noticed an exchange of special knowing between the women wrapped in long aprons, as they waited for the one called Mary Elizabeth to continue. Sophie wished she understood but she felt only confusion. Too much damage from the outside world remained.

The one called Mary reached for the next piece of Sophie's world. A thin light blanket with many small holes came away. "This piece has a name, actually two. It represents theft and greed, both foul enemies crushed along each thread. There is also a thread or two of guilt." Mary turned her head to breathe. "It was taken, actually stolen when needed by another."

Sophie's skin blanched and her head snapped up. Whatever she was called, the tall, beautiful lady would be the one to watch, the one to fear.

Mary waited, pain evident once again across her brow.

Sophie watched the flash of pain as she remembered slipping the blanket off a sleeping soul long ago. Yes, she had stolen the blanket thinking she needed the shabby piece more than the other. But how could this woman so many months later know?

Small signals, almost too small to notice, passed from Mary to the others as they placed the discarded items out of sight. Sophie did not understand what was happening but caught the exchanges.

A glimpse of insight would show in small ways how the women should proceed while causing no harm. They watched for a small shrug or flinching back of this new one in Abba's home, a drawing away in fear when gently touched. The goal of the three women here was to do no harm to each new one that came to them, all so different, different scars, different needs. Compassion filled the room.

Sophie watched the two women helpers who seemed to marvel at Mary's gift of insight even though they knew her.

Sophie felt waves of weakness and hoped to hold the roiling sickness down. Her stomach was empty for far too long, all of her surroundings too new, too unreal. Now the weakness tried to sweep over her again. When this degradation would finally be finished was anyone's guess. If an opportunity came to escape, she would run. As fast and far as she could. The only problem, she simply did not have the strength to move much less run.

Still weak and hoping not to be sick, a new thought settled. Maybe this chance really could be some sort of a new beginning. Followed instantly by another thought, *"No, it is some kind of trap"*. Sophie lived through enough entanglements to know traps were everywhere. She felt she would know if and when to escape so she reasoned it might not matter much if she stayed for a time. Maybe she could gain new strength. Sophie felt her lips curl slightly. She didn't believe in new beginnings. Somehow that dream died along the way. *Let them pluck me clean, I will survive.*

With a new resolve to run as soon as strength returned, Sophie began to let some of her muscles loosen. No need to decide anything now. Slowly a different feeling filtered in, too much happened in so few hours. Something new. Unsure of what she was feeling she let confusion engulf her.

Mary handed a heavy sweater to Monika, "this piece is full of jealousy. It is especially rank. Take care when putting it in the basket to be destroyed". A lower section of the piece was covered with green mold and created a foul stench.

Mary spoke again, barely heard, "When wrapped in jealousy, its tentacles reach deeper than one could imagine. It grows as wild vines grow and tries to reach deeper and further with the hope of finding even more fertile ground to pull into its web of misery."

Sophie's hands jerked to pull the sweater back to clasp against her chest. She remembered clearly when and where the sweater came from. How could this total stranger in this unworldly place possibly know?

The sweater was large and heavy and once belonged to a large woman who befriended Sophie. The woman fed the homeless girl and tried to help her, hoping to lift her out of the morass the girl had fallen into. But Sophie grew to resent the woman and her daughter for their constant way of doing things. And for obviously loving each other more than they cared for the outsider.

Oh! they tried, acted like they cared but she let her resentment for their pitiful, boring lives build until she knew it was time to leave. She made a way of escape, never to see either of them again but not before taking the woman's favorite sweater along with a couple of other things to barter later.

Sophie knew it was the woman's favorite sweater because the woman often expressed her love for it and the pleasure it brought her. Sophie watched the one called Mary put the sweater in the trash basket and felt the tear leak out of her eye and drip down to her chin. She wiped at her chin, thinking, *'Now what would cause that?'*

CHAPTER 9

Monika and Bridget nodded their understanding without actually looking at the girl as Mary continued to gently disrobe the stranger. Next Mary handed them a lighter piece of clothing a man's sweater. "Envy is subtle, but a very efficient destroyer. Take care not to touch it. Use the wooden tongs."

Sophie blinked while remaining quietly defeated as the sweater came gently down her arms, slipping off. Envy? Yes, it wasn't so much about him as it was about the other girl. Her clothing, her way of talking with friends, all of them from homes Sophie could never hope to be invited into. The places they enjoyed she could never afford and even if she could pay the price, she would never be accepted. She would never feel comfortable in their company. They were born with status, with standing in society. She was not, the chasm could not be breached.

Sophie remembered yearning to be included, but never was and probably would have hated it if she had been invited into their circle. The sweater gave little comfort the first cold nights she wore it after keeping the young man's sweater. It was left with her by mistake. It might have been easily returned to him or to his true love. The sweater never held the warmth she longed for, hoped for but she kept it because she could. Nothing ever turned out as she imagined it would.

How could this one called Mary know these secret things? This strange woman with this gift should be avoided in the future. Sophie felt her head begin to pound. Her world seemed upside down.

Bridget spoke softly, "I remember the first time you directed us to use the tongs." At the time Mary's look and tone had been direct and yet distant, almost forbidding. Now, Mary nodded at Bridget, probably remembering the moment in the past as well.

Mary, with steady hands, carefully removed a shirt with buttons missing, saying, "Use the tongs with this piece also. Here is a combination of lust and sexual sins". Mary sighed, placing the piece of filth on the extended wooden rod, pain seen on her features. Moments passed before Mary spoke, "This will have to be burned." The tall woman's voice held enough quiet authority to cause Monika and Bridget to quickly obey, reaching to place it in a burning container.

Perhaps as an afterthought, Mary added, "some garments are difficult to destroy even with fire."

Understanding, Monika held the wooden rod steady while Bridget pulled the large burn container closer.

Sophie willed herself to stone, hearing but not wanting to hear. Not letting her mind take her to places she could not bear to go. A strange unfamiliar pain washed through her body. Sophie trembled.

Seeming to understand, Mary continued in her soft clear voice, as though she was alone, "Now the skirt must be removed and then the foot wraps and leggings."

The one called Mary stooped to remove the scraps of laced leather and rags on Sophie's feet. The frightened girl gasped and drew back when Mary touched her feet. Such a plethora of emotions both from Sophie and Mary could be felt by the two small women assisting. Pain etched for a moment on Mary's lovely countenance before dissolving once again to calm. The skirt loosened, easily fell to the floor.

With a slight smile of reassurance, Mary handed the almost naked girl a large warm towel to wrap in and motioned for Sophie to sit on the stool positioned by the steaming tub of water and remove her stockings. There was little if any resemblance between the threads and holes removed from the thin legs to actual stockings.

Finally disrobed and wrapped in the warm towel, Sophie felt her nakedness. She heard Mary's soft definite words as the strange lady named the latest items removed.

"These final pieces are low self-esteem and self-pity, they are very sad little pieces. They are joined by some fear." Pointing to the girls' feet, "See the many small cuts and scars on her legs and ankles caused by fear?" Mary remained quiet for so long, the helpers wondered if there was something they should do, then as though speaking to herself, Mary sighed, "Fear has so many facets, so many ways of wounding, of destroying."

This person, this Mary Elizabeth, ripped Sophie to shreds with every description. These descriptions of her things had been, and probably still were Sophie's world.

Hoping it did not show, Sophie felt pure hatred for this woman called Mary Elizabeth. It ripped through her in a torrent of rage. Who did she think she was? The woman was obviously rich. And beautiful. Who would not be! Living in a castle, her every need and desire quickly fulfilled!! Sophie let her hatred boil up. Her mind began to devise ways to become enriched while here in this place before she ran. She would take all she could carry and make a new start as a new, well set-up person.

Her rage began to dissolve as her new plan formed. Sophie felt certain fairness in the thought before a moment of doubt crept in and shook the girls thinking. Bewilderment pushed against the hatred.

CHAPTER 10

Mary Elizabeth gave Monika and Bridget a nod, "Nothing is to be saved. Be sure we have adequate replacements for everything. All of it."

Sophie yanked her body back, tried to move out of the woman's reach. Mary did not move. She sat silent for a moment before she spoke. "It is warm and safe here. It is not a prison. You are free to leave at any time." Taking a small breath, she continued, "We will replace all that has been taken from you here this night and keep you warm and fed as long as you choose to remain with us but it will be up to you."

Sophie felt her anger shift. She felt unsure. She knew it wasn't wise to trust, it would only come to pain in the end. But she had to admit it did feel good to be warm. The woman seemed sincere but Sophie wasn't sure about the part of being safe. Still, Sophie felt the bile of hatred dissolve. Hope welled up within her for an instant, as it had so many times in the past before it turned to rejection or worse. Did she dare hope? With a small shrug of surrender, Sophie could only wonder, *What have I to lose?*

This Mary Elizabeth person appeared different than most people encountered through the past difficult months. Out there in the dark, in so many different unfamiliar places Sophie survived for as long or longer than most. Or so she believed. *Surviving* was not quite the right word but nothing else fit in her thinking at this moment. The past few weeks could not be called living. The cold, the hunger, the fear as she moved slowly toward death day after day through the winter months. With cool water and warm broth, Sophie's thoughts began to clear.

The gentle compassion in the eyes of the beautiful lady moved Sophie and a feeling of calm she could not hold back, even if she wanted to, moved across her heart. Able to think a bit more clearly, she decided there was no reason to bolt, at least not yet. The weary vagabond decided to trust this new possible kindness for a time. After all, just a few hours ago she was near certain death. With no one in sight to give her a cup of water much less treat her with kindness. Now refreshed with both food and drink a crack opened somewhere deep inside her bruised heart.

The woman called Mary could see the fear move out and a small portion of acceptance move into the wretched person. "Ah we are halfway there", speaking barely above a whisper, perhaps to herself, Mary smiled, holding out her hand. Sophie reached out to take the hand, the offered kindness.

"We are going to help you," Mary explained in a clear soft voice, "we will leave the things you no longer need, help you with bathing and replace all that you feel you are losing today with new possessions."

Then the woman chuckled, "We will make exchanges. We will replace all you feel you have lost and perhaps some good will emerge from the bargain we make today."

Monika's foot tapped a restless click, tap, tap, as she tried not to scowl. Tired of waiting for this moment, she said, "Well, can we finally get about the bathing before the water turns lukewarm?"

Mary understood Monika's need to be about other tasks. Soon it would be dawn. The small woman always carried a list of things needing her attention. Most folks in the castle were familiar with a tap or two of her foot, trying to move things along. Mary smiled at her worthy assistant, saying, "all things in good time."

Standing back with Bridget, Monika watched as the newest member moved gently into the castle family and permitted the one called Mary to remove the last of her personal filth. Reaching back to hand Bridget the last pieces to be placed in the basket of waste, Mary caught the questioning looks from the two small women and shook her head and repeated, "Nothing is to be saved."

Sophie heard and a small gasp escaped, but she held her tongue as she listened to the woman's murmur. All of her things, her trusted companions against the cold days and colder nights and so much more, being pitched, thrown away, taken to be burned. They were leaving nothing for her to cling to.

Mary spoke of the last scraps taken, (more to herself than others), as she lifted them to her helpers. "These last are pieces soaked and dried in anger and a lying spirit along with other things that wound." Thoughtful, Mary continued, "Hurt feelings must heal. The healing process can happen quickly if one is willing. Some wounds are often slower to heal than broken bones, but that need not be true."

Bridget said, "Yes, what the eyes can't see can be the worst." Both Monika and Bridget understood that Mary could have remained silent. Instead, she shared her gift of seeing into realms others were not privy to. It was her wonderful way of teaching laced with compassion. They loved her and felt honored when asked to work with her. This night was no different.

The disrobing was now completed, one piece at a time until the neck, arms and legs were in clear view. Monika's eyes filled with tears ready to brim over at the visible damage done to the young woman's flesh. No matter how many times she helped with this final part of the process of giving comfort to a new one, Monika still found it difficult to scrub off the filth, then treat the obvious wounds with healing ointments. She always felt a wrenching pain in her own being, knowing this could happen to anyone. A pure love for the new one, safely out of the cold, filled Monika's heart. It pushed the little woman's impatience aside for now.

CHAPTER 11

Mary often spoke of pains that are hard to discount in the beginning before the healing and joy come. Some scars last. It would take more than one bath and one change of clothes to see what kind of person might emerge.

The warm towel remained wrapped around Sophie as she waited. Her anger now gone, she felt nothing. Resigned and confused she would endure whatever came next.

Mary motioned for a folded ornate screen to be placed near the tub to provide privacy for Sophie so she could remove the warm towel and step into the tub.

"Ah, thank goodness the water is still warm." nodding, Monika said, "Please get into the water so we can finish."

The three waited, heard a splash and a long sigh, before peeking around the screen to be sure all was well. Then the task of scrubbing the half-starved human from head to toe began in earnest.

Sophie did not resist. The warm water, fragrant soap, and gentle hands soothed her. She let every fiber begin to unwind as she felt a trace of defeat but also found it wonderful to be full of broth and covered with warm almost hot water.

Sophie wondered if she could be dreaming. This surely must be some strange fantasy soon to come to an end. She sighed again and again, letting herself relax completely. Things were turned inside out and upside down this entire night since she first curled around the lamp post in a round circle of light. Maybe the streetlamp held magical powers. She heard stories of such things, mostly from time spent with an Irish family last year. She felt too deliciously peaceful to think about it, perhaps later but for now she would savor the wonder of this night.

Bridget and Monika laid out the chosen garments for Sophie. "Time to finish and dress, just in time for a small repast. We will take a moment to say good-night to others before the last of the lamps are turned low." Mary's voice remained soft as she held up a fresh towel. "It is getting late. I believe all here have experienced a day to remember." The two small helpers chuckled.

The fresh towel now wrapped around Sophie held an unfamiliar warmth. And again, she was surrounded by the incredible fragrance that filled the air. The freshly scrubbed girl looked up into Mary's face and wasn't sure she could speak loud enough to be heard. "Thank you."

The slender, graceful woman called Mary dried her hands and said, "You are more than welcome." Sophie watched and waited to see what came next, catching a glimpse of humor, or something very like humor in the woman's eyes.

Looking around Sophie felt a whole new range of emotions. Emotions she could not identify, leaving her bereft, like a small ship without an anchor on a roiling sea.

Sophie filled her lungs with warmth, trying to relax as she remained silent and let the women treat her wounds before beginning the process to replace all that had been taken from her. Looking down at her body Sophie found it odd to see sores on her arms and legs. Numbed by life these past few weeks, her body failed to alert her of the deterioration of her flesh.

Mary and the others dressed the wounds with care and all hands touching her were soft and kind. Sophie's eyes filled with unwanted tears again, unable to remember when she'd last cried. Of course, there had been times in the past when she wept. But when? The tenderness she longed for throughout her life, now freely given by strangers, suddenly overwhelmed her.

Sophie's thoughts shifted. '*Take what you can and give nothing in return might not be the only way to live after all.*' This clear new thought fell into an empty space in her heart. But should she, did she dare to hope?

A lovely light blue gown of material unfamiliar to Sophie slipped over her head and was fastened with a ribbon at her waist. Monica tied the white sash and Mary placed a small gray cape over Sophie's shoulders. Her clean hair was plaited in braids and wrapped around her head, tightly held in place with small combs encrusted with blue stones. Sophie glanced down and could see she was dressed much like the others and marveled at the miracle. "Whose things are these? Did the person die?"

Monika poked her tongue out of the side of her mouth and winked at Mary, making Mary laugh before she answered, "No these were here just for you. You will understand in time." Tipping her head down for a moment, Mary said, "Come, we shall eat. You must be hungry."

Sophie watched as Mary and the other two removed their aprons, folded them and set them aside. Sophie noticed the layers of beautiful fabric cascading in a gentle way from Mary's empire waist to the floor as she turned. All three stood looking as though they had just walked in from a stroll in the garden. Sophie remembered thinking just an hour or so ago of taking what she could and giving nothing in return. But perhaps there might be another, better way to live. This clear new thought fell into her heart. Sophie wondered if a new life *could* be possible.

"I believe we are now ready to go to the dining hall." The four women walked down a passageway turning into a large open area. Looking to her left Sophie watched reflections in tall mirrors placed along the wall, at first not realizing the reflection of the pretty young woman dressed in blue seemed familiar. The dark hair dressed in jeweled combs, hazel eyes with curled lashes, clear and clean complexion seemed somehow familiar. Nothing about this soft appearing creature whose reflection she watched could ever understand the world outside of this castle. The person in the mirror would not have the strength it takes to survive out there in a world where Sophie herself had lived for so long.

Looking again into the mirror, Sophie noted her reflection, thinking 'I do not belong here'. A lovely young woman stared back, *but this is not me, this is not me.* She wanted to scream the words out loud.

Sophie turned from the mirror and walked across the room to where she found Mary settled at a small table just big enough for two. The food looked wonderful. Sophie joined Mary; her lovely gown spread around her. They quietly enjoyed their light meal together, all of it unreal to Sophie. Depictions of the rich life she read about drew her and her long ago dream came and filled her again. She imagined such luxury and comfort for herself many times but her dreams never materialized. Now here in this place, in this room, the people, the food, the soft music all seemed so real! She could taste the food, enjoy the cool drink. Dark images from the past floated up to caution her to be careful. It was not, could not be her world!

The spacious hall gleamed with flickering candle lights and fresh flowers in lovely vases on all of the small tables. The laughter from others touched Sophie with a new sharp pang of longing. She felt a swarm of new emotions. All around her laughter seemed to fill the air. The room was filled with people who seemed to pay little attention to Sophie as they continued to converse and laugh softly. The hour was late and some were quietly leaving.

Sophie looked around at the others before turning to Mary. She snapped, "Why are you being so kind? You don't know me." As an afterthought she added, "I do not need anyone." Sophie spoke quickly, keeping her eyes on her plate of food, realizing how foolish she must sound.

Mary smiled, "It is a pleasure to help you. Perhaps understanding will come. What does it matter today as long as you are warm and safe? And with food enough to drive out hunger, at least for tonight.

Sophie did not look up but agreed with a nod of her head, "Good food and being warm *is* better than being cold and starving." She felt the corner of her lips twitch and turn up. Breathing in the mingled fragrances, she let a bite of warm roll with butter melt in her mouth and Sophie truly relaxed for the first time in recent memory.

"I hope you and I will become good friends. Abba does care for all of us and always hopes the new ones like yourself will stay at least until they are completely well and strong." Mary took a bite of roll, waited, "Change is difficult for some people, but change comes whether for good or bad. I would love to be a part of a good outcome for you. Can you understand that?"

"I think I can. It takes more than a bath, a change of clothes and a plate of food to cause real change." Sophie felt the old anger bubble up from deep inside. Her eyes were full of suspicion she hoped to hide. '*This simply is not going to work. I will run as soon as I am able. I do not belong here, I never will.*'

Mary watched Sophie's expressions change and seemed to understand.

"Let us enjoy our meal and think about all the questions later, shall we?"

"Of course."

Sophie watched as Mary smiled, that same distant look in the beautiful woman's eyes. Sophie bent over her plate, hoping to trample down her constant hunger at least for now, as she tried to embrace this new world around her, at least for the night.

Mary remained silent eating her fruit slowly. Yes, there was work to be done but she would find a way to convey the wonder of possibilities for this new young one who a few hours ago lay huddled against a lamppost near death and completely without hope.

Mary looked across into a world that only she could see and felt the thrill, the wonder of it from each new one who came to Abba's estates. Mary recalled the early days at the castle when she first came, still young and so lost, before growing, learning, being accepted, becoming useful. Some memories stayed as reminders, memories that never left her. The best part of all of it came gradually, as she became a small part of the changed lives of others. The lives of the broken ones who were found and brought or those who came on their own through the gates. Each one could become a part of the peace and freedom offered here or leave when they were stronger. It was always their choice but Mary worked to help those who struggled make the right choice for their lives

CHAPTER 12

Mary remembered feeling like a sponge her first weeks here, soaking up all the newly felt peace around her. She felt loved, protected, and needed here from the very beginning. Abba blessed her efforts, knowing she made a difference in those she helped. Mary Elizabeth knew there was much still to learn. And the learning itself gave life purpose. She remembered hearing that one should never stop growing in wisdom and understanding.

Abba taught her to be guided by good, one day at a time. Always reminding her there would be time for all her dreams to be fulfilled, no need to rush. Mary trusted his words.

Both women sat quietly finishing their meal. Without appearing to, Sophie searched Mary's face. She'd caught the faraway look in the beautiful woman's eyes a moment ago. Was the woman hiding something if so what and what could it have to do with her? Sophie prided herself on being alert, staying vigilant and aware of her surroundings, especially those around her. Yet she struggled tonight to understand.

Realizing there appeared no need to rush, Sophie made a conscious decision to wait, find an opening, a safe time to leave, carefully prepare, and be on her way at a time of her choosing. She would watch and learn. Nothing felt right here. It must be a trap, a very attractive trap but a trap no less.

Sophie admitted it felt really good to be clean and well rested, and no longer haunted by hunger. With fear held at bay, at least for now, perhaps she could find a quiet place in her mind and take time to sort things out. She had no way of knowing for how long they would be kind. What did they want from her? She had nothing. They were surely more aware of her situation than even she understood. In the beginning, she ran before she knew how to survive. She was older now and much wiser. As new, clear thoughts came, she felt her confidence returning. She would not make the same mistakes she'd made in the beginning. Her thoughts would surely clear even more with daily food and fresh water. Perhaps she could stay here at the castle and learn, be more prepared to find what she searched for once she was on her own again. The rich life was out there. She was sure she could find it once she felt stronger.

The image of the reflection she'd seen in the huge hall mirror crossed her mind. With the right clothes and better nutrition, she might still accomplish her goals, find the position and riches she knew she deserved. If the reflection was anywhere near the truth, she was still young and very pretty.

Yes, a few hours ago she longed for death, but her fortunes seemed to have changed. With cautious optimism, Sophie felt the winds of change turning toward a future she deserved. These new thoughts pleased Sophie. She would take advantage of the opportunity offered here in this strange place and learn to be a lady accepted in high places. Another impossible dream? Maybe not. This could be the help she needed all along to get what she deserved; a new life full of all life had to offer.

Wonderful images tumbled through her. Sophie mulled one possibility after another about how long to stay and when to choose a proper time for leaving. Leave or wait, take a few days, or maybe longer and see how things are done in this place. She knew she was a quick study, could watch and learn to be a lady like Mary Elizabeth. She *could* do that. A temporary arrangement to be sure, she could have giggled. She felt so full of hope. Things that just a few hours ago seemed totally impossible now seemed within her reach.

It was not the first bath she ever enjoyed nor the first good meal. But she had to admit the last of either must have been many weeks ago. Her decision, now firmly made, she would wait. It would take time but living in these comfortable conditions should afford her the time and opportunity to become a lady. It might take weeks, even months. What did it matter as long as her goal became her new reality?

Sophie suddenly became weak with the excitement, knowing she still needed to heal. She must not rush. The decision made, she would stay for now, and certainly never go back to her old life. Never! Earlier wrong turns taken had almost destroyed her. She would stay here as long as possible. Until a firm plan unfolded. She must be careful, stay alert, use all that she learned from the past, and see where all of this led. Hopefully toward a bright future.

The one called Mary was like no one Sophie ever knew, such a compassionate being, and gifted, also she appeared to be a very strong person. Why would she bother caring for a stranger? A filthy, sick stranger? What reward could there possibly be for one who looked and behaved like royalty in taking on such a task?

Sophie wondered if the original stench covering her a few hours ago, could really be gone.

Sophie shifted her gaze to look around the dining hall. As she and Mary finished their meal in peaceful silence, each thinking private thoughts as music softened and lamps dimmed. Sophie tried to cover a yawn. She relaxed and let weariness settle through her.

The meal finished, Mary's hand touched Sophie's elbow, "Let's go meet some others before we find your bed." After meeting a few people, Mary led Sophie into another part of the huge castle. Whatever else it might be it was indeed a castle, perhaps the largest in the whole world! Sophie found herself breathless rounding each corner, down each passageway, seeing new riches and beauty in every space.

As the two women found their way to sleeping quarters, Sophie could not remember the name of a single person she met earlier, except maybe Henri, and his friend Max (short for Maximilian). Max appeared different in every way from his friend Henri. The twinkle in his eye, mischievous, yes that is what she saw! Alarms! She'd be on guard with that one! He boldly winked at her when introduced.

Sophie smiled remembering. It was not the first time she'd been flirted with or winked at but surprised and unexpected at this time, in this place. Thinking back on meeting the two friends, Sophie remembered the tall, gentle Henri. He helped prepare her bath earlier but didn't appear to recognize her later in the dining hall.

She knew he did not remember her. How could he, she being so completely covered when she first arrived, not to mention being wrapped in filth? The stench must have been difficult for the one called Henri and for the others. Sophie was grateful they did not remember her. Her hands were still very rough but she felt the transformation from filthy waif to the clean, well-dressed person seen in the reflection just an hour ago amazing. She could only marvel at the change. The others in the dining hall didn't notice, or did they? Were there snickers and retorts behind her back?

Sophie shrugged, knowing she arrived here against her will and would leave when ready. Until then she would watch, learn, and prepare to leave quickly if necessary.

Once tucked in a small soft bed Mary bid Sophie good night. Wrapped in warm blankets drenched in the fragrance of lavender, Sophie was asleep before the door closed behind Mary Elizabeth.

"What a lovely morning!" Mary moved across the small room to draw back a heavy drape and open a window, letting a fresh breeze blow into the room. Sophie threw an arm across her eyes to shut out the bright light before peeking out, seeing Mary smiling down at her. How could anyone be so lovely and wide awake so early in the day?

How long had she slept? Must have been hours. The wonder of the late morning sun drenching the room captured Sophie. No one entered the room during the night to hurt or disturb her. No bone-chilling cold intruded, no terrible dreams forced her awake during the dark hours.

Sophie let the ache of peace fill her as she felt the warmth of the morning sun. She closed her eyes to feel these new emotions. Whatever should come next, she knew her body and her mind were well-rested for the first time in many days.

"Are you ill? Is there something I can fetch for you? This woman actually seemed concerned! The thought of Mary *fetching* anything for Sophie caused the girl's eyes to open wide and lips to curl in a slight smile.

"Ah, I knew there was a beautiful smile there waiting to come out." With a motion for the new arrival to follow, Mary led Sophie from her bed to a wardrobe, saying, "Come let us be about dressing for our day ahead. There are many things to be done today."

Not understanding any of it, Sophie did as asked, changing out of her nightdress she washed in the freshwater on the nightstand. She watched Mary pick a dress and slippers from the large armoire before seating her in front of a mirror to dress her hair. Mary worked wonders pulling the mass of unruly strands into place with several small combs. Sophie was mesmerized as she watched the process, amazed at the final results.

Soon the two were once again in the dining hall eating small biscuits and fruit. As they enjoyed their food and drank hot tea, Mary suddenly asked, "Do you want to change?"

Sophie lifted the biscuit, her brow creased, "Change? I have changed. Yesterday I wore blue. Today you gave me a yellow gown to wear."

Sophie paused, her brow creased, looking down, "Whose clothes are these anyway?" Not waiting for an answer, she watched Mary's expression alter as her mind flashed back to the question just asked. "Change? How do you mean?" Sophies, honest confusion could not be mistaken. This young woman, new to the castle and all it offered, straightened, becoming very still, her eyes holding something close to anger.

Mary bent toward her new charge, understanding how different things must seem to her here and now.

"Abba found you in rather dire straits. My friends and I threw out some of your old life, made you comfortable and made it possible for you to rest. Now I need to know what we should do next, you and me? What are your hopes? Do you desire a different life from the one left behind yesterday?"

Sophie's thoughts swirled as she fought for understanding. No one ever asked her these questions before. The concept of someone caring to ask now came so new she couldn't respond.

Mary smiled, "First let me tell you that you are not a prisoner here nor are you compelled in any way to remain here with me, with us. You are completely free to go, leave at any time of your choosing.

Sophie's thoughts spun. *'Free to leave. Leave at any time.'* That is what the one called Mary said. I can leave today. A frown came and went as Sophie considered. But why not stay, glean all she could from this woman, this place. Go at the time of her own choosing, as first planned. Sophie began to relax once the decision to stay for now was reached.

Smiling a slight smile, Mary spoke, "If you choose to stay with us there will be work. We have many things that need our attention. You may wish to help, but it is up to you. Perhaps the first thing you need to know is this is a place of peace and hope. A place where you may hope for a worthwhile life full of love."

Mary paused to gaze out of the open doorway of the dining hall, "A first step will be to show you what life here looks and feels like, show you that in many ways love is something you do, not just something you feel."

"I expect most of your life has been filled with feelings, yours or someone else's. Hunger, loneliness, thirst, physical pain. And some good feelings, some joy, perhaps some happy memories. I should think there were some truly bad times in the recent past, or I miss my guess. But that can end today if you are willing to trust others to help you make some changes, help plan a path forward to a different, better life." Mary's gaze never left Sophie's face.

This new form of attack caught Sophie off guard. She couldn't be sure how to respond so she remained silent.

CHAPTER 13

Their tea finished, the two left the hall. "Come let us speak of these things outside in the garden." Mary slipped her hand under Sophie's arm as she guided them to a stone bench at the edge of the path. Mary settled on the bench, signalling Sophie to do the same. They spread their gowns around them as the sun seeped slowly across the gardens. Both soaked in the beautiful day.

Mary's brow creased as she considered a plan, a direction for this new friend. Each new one coming to the castle, especially the most devastated beings brought home by Abba himself, came with different needs and wants that were often a challenge. Mary would need to be patient, seek to understand Sophie and talk with Abba about her before a more permanent plan could be put in place.

Sophie watched the woman closely. Perhaps she truly was one who could become a friend. She waited. *Is the pretty lady trying to figure out what to do with me, see if I am worthy of being helped? What comes next?*

A picture crossed Sophie's mind as she recalled seeing a potter in a slanted shelter under a tin roof along a lane. He took a lump of soft clay and gradually moulded it into a useful bowl. Then came the fire! Sophie shrugged, thinking she wouldn't make much of a bowl!

A smile crept across Sophie's face as the vision of thumbs and palms, dripping with water, worked over the clay on the potter's wheel, trying to make something worthwhile out of *her*.

She sighed, knowing she looked much like the others that surrounded her this morning, but she knew her heart, and it was unchanged. Sophie was no longer hungry, and the loneliness abated, at least for now. But she felt exactly the same in her heart as she did a few days ago. A smirk crossed before it dissolved. She hoped Mary could not see into her thoughts. Sophie knew she did not fit here in this extraordinary place, would never be a real part of the peace permeating the very air she now breathed.

The old familiar resolve settled in. She would take one day at a time. There could be no way of knowing how long this new existence would last. She would stay for now but be ready to leave at a moment's notice. For years the girl had moved in and out of hunger, of lack, accepting much of it as a part of life. Her mother's life and now hers. Wasn't that the way life worked, had always worked? Always feast or famine. The girl understood clearly what waited for her outside of the castle - more hunger like ravenous wolves. Cold and lack waited for her to return to her real life. Let them wait! At least for now. Once her decision was made, Sophie began to relax in the garden, feeling the warmth of the morning sun.

After resting quietly for a time, Mary rose from the bench and extended her hand, "I enjoyed our lovely biscuits and tea this morning." Turning to look out over the endless gardens, she said, "Come, I would like to show you the grounds surrounding the castle."

Sophie followed without complaint along the pathway, through trees and gardens beginning to overflow with color. As they walked the stone paths, Mary pointed out and gave names to lovely blooms. Sophie felt tears brim, ready to overflow at the sheer beauty around her. Though a chill still hung in the air, the spring weather and the new blooms were a gift to be treasured.

Walking through the gardens filled Sophie with something more than wonder. No words came to describe how she felt. *An ache, a really good ache.* Yes, a rainbow of color filled her senses. Sophie began to enjoy every minute spent with this gentle woman who now walked with her and spoke of new beginnings. She could not hold back this new calm joy that began to fill all the empty spaces.

A warning slipped in, *'be careful'*, before dissolving into distant mist. Unsure what to call it, Sophie knew this feeling was different than any felt before. She smiled; ache was not the appropriate description for what she felt but would have to do for now.

Taking a breath, Sophie asked, "What fragrance fills the air? It is the same pleasant scent in the room where I slept."

"The floral scent is named Lavender. Hereby the path is some not yet in bloom, it is too early. But you can see the long stems." Mary stood at the edge of the path. The delicate soft blooms were partially opened in an array of light and darker shades of purple strung along the garden path.

"Lavender, a lovely name. So very…" Sophie paused, unable to put her own description to the lovely slender plants. Looking out across the acres of vivid colors of every hue just beginning to meet Spring, the girl whispered, "How can there be such beauty in one place?" Lips suppressed, eyes ready to spill tears down her cheeks, the girl deprived of beauty most of her days stood silent, barely moving her head.

Mary remembered her first visit to the gardens so long ago and understood much of what Sophie must be feeling.

Sophie whispered, "How can one bear more beauty than we see here today?" She tried to take in all of the beauty surrounding her. As they walked through the gardens, some of the areas were smaller and less structured than others, Sophie gazed at the rolling hills in the distance. Hills used for growing vegetables, all manner of plants and trees. Mary shared many things about the castle grounds as they walked. Sophie marveled at such abundance when so much of the country she recently traveled through was barren, gardens producing little this last season. Certainly not enough to feed a family through the winter season.

The two women, slowly learning each other's ways, spent the rest of the morning on the castle grounds. As they turned back toward the castle, Mary asked, "Sophie, do you have questions, anything you wish to ask me?"

Sophie's brow creased, considering, wondering if she dared ask half the questions now rushing through her mind. Sophie lowered her head before looking up at the one called Mary, "Why do you call the king of this place Abba?"

"Because that is his name. You will learn much more about Abba in time. Is there anything else?"

"Why did he fetch me out of the night? How did he know I was there?" Sophie seemed to ponder all of it, "Why would anyone care on such a night when doors were being bolted against the night?" She paused, "Who are you and why are you here, being more than kind to a stranger?"

The dam of loneliness shifted inside the girl and the questions came out in a torrent before an answer could be formed. Tears threatened as Sophie stopped to gasp for air. She felt the arm wrap around her shoulders and without understanding why, she let herself fold into Mary Elizabeth's cloak.

Sophie could not hold back the tears. The soft touch brought racking sobs, too long held inside. She turned slowly into Mary's embrace until the sob's began to subside. Mary wiped the dampness away with her kerchief as the weeping gradually slowed. Leading Sophie to a nearby bench, the women settled into a cocoon of silence and let the healing balm in this open sanctuary work yet another miracle.

More hours passed as the two talked softly of many things through the noon hour. Mary answered each question asked. The answers seemed to satisfy, at least for now.

CHAPTER 14

"What kind of work do you like to do?" Mary, nodding to others in passing, asked as the two returned to the castle. Looking at the others going about, Sophie asked, "What do all of these others do?" Her expression was so serious, before looking down, "I do nothing, at least not well. You might as well know that now!"

"Perhaps, but how do you know what you might be capable of?" Mary chuckled, "We will take time to discover the real Sophie."

Ah yes, time. It takes time for a new acquaintance to become a trusted friend, even longer before sharing personal confidences. The real Sophie! Who is she and how do 'we' uncover the 'real' person?

Mary watched as confusion came and went, before falling again across the girl's face. Smiling, she said, "One day at a time, one task at a time. For instance, do you like children? Or do you prefer to be busy outside, away from children? Do you think of yourself as a patient, forgiving person? Do you think of yourself as a 'natural' frowner or of one with an easy smile?"

Each question put before Sophie came with kindness unfamiliar to the girl.

"I suppose one of the most important questions today should be a question for the heart." Mary paused, "Are you willing to find out who you can become?"

The questions through the hour came slowly. No answers were needed as Mary watched Sophie consider each question. As the two strolled through the gardens, Mary felt the girl start to consider a better way. Drawing near to one of the side entrances, both women knew many questions would have to wait to be answered.

"It is time to go in." Sophie felt the warmth of Mary's smile and a truth she hesitated to trust. Perhaps a friend? Did she dare to believe? At times, in the past, her loneliness conjured a friend from pictures and stories she read and remembered. But here today someone actually offered friendship. And not just anyone, but the beautiful Mary Elizabeth. The thought left a knot in Sophie's stomach.

"Tomorrow we will be about Abba's business. We will see how you find living among those with true regard for others who are living their lives here."

The next few days passed in a blur as a new kind of peace and a measure of excitement she did not understand enveloped Sophie. The concept of receiving a lasting peace that Mary often spoke of overwhelmed the girl. That would truly be a miracle and Sophie did not believe in miracles!

At the beginning of Sophie's second week, Mary led her to a large room, unseen by the girl earlier in her tours around the castle. Sophie let her gaze sweep the large space, a gasp escaping. Such a large room, quiet but full of sunlight from long windows on the east and south sides of the room. Soft rugs lay under small tables with chairs and benches for comfort scattered about. And books! Shelves and shelves of books, hundreds of them! Sophie forgot to breathe as she turned to take in the entire room.

Mary whispered, "Our library is always open, you may come anytime you like, as long as your duties are performed and daily tasks are finished."

"So many books," Sophie walked to a nearby shelf and ran her fingers over spines, most titles unknown to her. When she found one familiar, she brightened, as though seeing again an old acquaintance. Smiling, she was unable to stop joy from bubbling up.

Mary left Sophie's side and walked to a small writing desk near a window. "Please make yourself comfortable. I have some things needing my attention, so we will be here for a couple of hours." Mary spoke softly as she removed a book from one of the shelves and returned to the desk, picked up a quill before removing a sheet of parchment from the desk drawer and bent over the open book.

Sophie watched her friend for a few minutes, as Mary continued to turn pages of the large book. Mary seemed to search, and find what she was looking for before searching further, more pages turning. Mary returned to the book-lined shelves from time to time to search for yet another volume.

Sophie left Mary seated in the light to explore and seek out a new treasure for herself. Sophie slowly walked the entire room, soaking in the feel, the smell of this new paradise. Finding first one familiar title, then a second, she finally chose a book of children's stories. A gift she would enjoy today, knowing she would come often to this place. She pushed down a twinge of guilt. She could offer nothing in return so fine, so heartwarming as the library. Such a gift, freely given. Little was asked of her with only kindness shown to her. A few weeks ago, she could not have imagined such a place as she now enjoyed. And now, today all the books she could ever hope to read and enjoy were shelved before her.

Sophie's life seemed packed with so much newness it was difficult to grasp. People to meet, much to learn. She made a conscious decision to find her place in Abba's world, to work, learn, try to trust. And read until her eyes rebelled! She laughed at the thought.

The old life, old ways of thinking gradually began to flake off in small ways, much of it more quickly than expected, but some of the dark still clung in the recesses of her being. Much as barnacles being painfully scrapped from her heart.

Mary often spoke of these things, and more. She said becoming a mature person felt much like carpenters and rock builders building a tall building from the depths up. The foundation seemed to be Mary's focus for days. When Sophie felt like a failure, Mary pointed out her many recent successes.

Mary spent time with Sophie and encouraged her daily to work toward a new and different life. Sophie understood some of the things Mary spoke of. She understood that life held promise, where a few weeks ago it held only fear and desperation. Even death.

Learning to live a completely different way was difficult in the beginning, often she felt very uncomfortable. When Sophie questioned, Mary would look up, think for a moment and then compare changes to small surgeries that would bring wholeness in time. As spring turned to summer Sophie began to bloom along with the gardens she loved. Her contentment lay like an aura over and around her.

CHAPTER 15

As the days passed and Sophie met many different people, two of her favorites became Henri, (who filled her bath on her first evening in the castle), and Max, (Maximillian), often seen at Henri's side. The two men usually chose tasks for the day they could do together. Henri lived a quiet, solemn, almost sad appearing existence. He stood tall, well over six feet and when she stood near him, she felt small. His slender frame towered over her, making it necessary to tip her face up when close to him. Which she tried to do every now and then to look into the bluest eyes ever seen, often full of gentle concern for something needed by a friend.

Henri was never outwardly jolly like his friend Max. But Sophie liked him the best. His short sandy colored hair framed his long oval shaped face. A face she would look for and loved to see, it wasn't difficult to find him among others due to his height. She loved his hands, his long, tapered fingers. Watching him from a distance, seeing how he held something, anything, she could feel tenderness in his movements. Never rash or crushing. Sophie spoke to him on rare occasions but she was sure he never noticed her.

Over the weeks Sophie also noticed the offhand way others paid their respect to the tall young man. Not sure why, but Sophie never thought to question what she felt or why. There was just something about the almost plain man that fascinated her. She watched him as he worked in the garden alone or at tasks with his friend, Max. Sophie noticed Henri always came quietly when called by Abba or Mary. Some tasks were difficult or unpleasant for Sophie. She marveled that Henri seemed to truly enjoy all of the work, any task no matter how difficult and Mary once mentioned that he preferred to be busy.

Often Henri appeared placid, neither kind nor unkind. Sophie tried to be more like this man she admired and was still able to remember his gentle ways the night she first arrived. He carefully gathered her and all her rags and carried her from the entrance to where Mary directed. Sophie knew Henri did not remember, but she did. She could recall the smallest of moments spent with the good young man.

It was different from Henri's friend Max. Sophie sensed a warning from their first encounter coupled with a trace of fear. Max, a young handsome man close to her own age, perhaps a few years older made her uncomfortable but she was at a loss to understand what she felt or why. Handsome and with a shameless grin, he winked at her on the eve of their first meeting but that was not her first wink. Still the sly smile and wink troubled her. He'd shown the same boldness toward her since that first encounter and she usually ignored him except for the one time she boldly winked back for a reaction. He tipped his dark curls and with a chuckle, walked on.

She remembered feeling shame for both Max and herself. It would never happen again. Max enjoyed the game, trying to lay a trap for an innocent. His arched brows and crooked reckless smile could be seen daily. Sophie began to realize Max meant no harm. Mary shared with Sophie that Max came from a dark place before coming into the peace he now enjoyed, this place where he now belonged. Still, at times Max seemed tethered to the darkness outside of the castle, something Sophie could not understand. She still knew she would leave, go find her fortune, but Max? Who could know what plans lay behind his smiles? Everyone accepted Max as a good soul, especially because of his friend, Henri. How else could the good man be best friends with someone so different from himself.

Henri protected his friend and seemed to hold Max in check in some way. Sophie did not know how to explain her thoughts to Mary concerning Max so she let it be. Max laughed at everything and nothing. He continued to smile his crooked smile and from time-to-time wink at any girl passing. One could only shrug and walk on. Everyone in truth accepted Max as he was, a handsome man with deep dimples and a blinding smile. Still, Sophie could not ignore the warnings or try to guess what kind of thoughts rattled around in his head at any given time.

Henri, the taller of the two by several inches would be slightly bent, his head tipped down nodding at something Max was sharing at the moment. Max with his dark head of curls tipped back to face his friend and his hands gesturing in all directions would cause Sophie to smile. At times Sophie watched without staring and longed for such a friendship of her own. On a level, she did not understand Sophie knew Mary Elizabeth could not be that friend. A friend and confidant to be sure but more a teacher and a guide than a close friend.

Early one morning Henri and Max came near, and Max called out to Mary and Sophie, "It is laundry day, and we choose you to be part of our scrub team today." Henri looked at Max and actually laughed, a rare thing indeed.

Sophie looked up at Mary, "Are they serious?"

Mary nodded, "I am afraid so. And since we *love* teamwork, they have decided to include us in their fun for the day. "Fun", Sophie watched as Mary wrapped her hand around the handle of one of the loaded baskets and headed off toward the back gardens with Henri.

Max smiled his slightly wicked smile and winked, "That leaves you and me to follow." Sophie shook her head in feigned disgust but could not hold back a slight grin.

The day was long and they worked hard but Henri and Max made it fun. The afternoon passed quickly. Others would come and gather in the dry laundry later. Sophie felt a bit of weariness but not Mary. She would have to ask her about that later. Mary seemed to have an endless reserve of energy no matter what the task. Sophie shrugged. So many questions, so much to learn!

CHAPTER 16

Each new day brought different lessons and new ways of thinking. The best part of any day were the long walks with Mary, usually in the late afternoon while sunlight still covered the gardens. Time propelled Sophie from one day into the next. Mary's gentle words of encouragement sprinkled throughout the quiet hours wrapped around the slender girl like a protective cloak as the days stretched into weeks and the weeks into months. Time brought change.

Sophie grew strong, both physically and mentally, and there were times when she could only remember the distant past when alone in her bed, and even then, the images were not clear. The young Sophie today held no resemblance to the young person who arrived here a few short months ago.

Sophie embraced this newness of life, slowly releasing the misery she brought with her. She treasured Mary's companionship and always swelled with a bit of pride when the two were together. Sophie knew she could never completely heal if separated from her mentor.

Beauty surrounded Mary with a soft mist of pure loveliness, which also encased Sophie when the two were together, she loved Mary and would stay beside her forever. Or so Sophie believed.

Late one warm August afternoon the two friends sat on the same bench where Sophie spent part of her first day at the castle with Mary some months ago. She remembered it was the first full day of Spring, the day after her first healing bath.

Both thinking their own thoughts now but somehow the silence felt different to Sophie. Mary began to speak and Sophie felt a difference in her tone. Without really listening she heard her mentor's soft words and her pulse quickened. The words were difficult for Sophie to assimilate on such a perfect day.

Mary smiled, "You have changed and grown in your time here. Though still young, I believe you to be a strong woman. I also believe you are ready to move to a new, higher level of responsibility. The king agrees."

"In your time here with us, you have become a part of a strong band of friends. Monika and Bridget and Darla, along with Henri and Max. Of course, there are others." Mary paused, folding her hands into the fabric of her skirt. She seemed unsure of how to proceed. Sophie held her breath and waited. "A fine group of friends to share your life with." Mary looked down again at her hands crossed in her lap.

"What are you saying?" Sophie's voice cracked. An alarm clearly heard, "Are you leaving? Are we to be separated?" Sophie felt the truth and once again the old familiar rejection folded through her. She became physically weak and willed herself to breathe. Feeling gut-wrenching fear for the first time in months, she felt a tear fall. The young woman wondered where this conversation was going as a piercing of the nearly forgotten painful times entered her heart. She knew there was more, felt the small shift and waited expressionless for what would come next.

Mary gazed at Sophie, willing the girl to meet her eyes. "I am not leaving. And I am here for you always. Anytime you should need me, but Abba has gathered in another soul, and has asked me to work with her and guide her into a new life." Minutes passed without words. "We have many who have joined us since you came, but most come of their own accord willingly, to find and live better lives but a few come directly here by the way of King Abba, in the same way you did. At certain times, Abba feels I am the best fit for the new broken one."

Someone needs you more than me! No! It is not possible! Sophie hoped her face revealed nothing of the torrent felt deep within her. Yes, I've changed. My body is healed, my mind has cleared, and I am busy with tasks I often enjoy, especially my time in the library. There is always some work to be done there but my joy is complete when I am among so many great books.

Her thoughts swung back to the present moment. '*I love you, I need you. I thought we were friends!* These thoughts and more reeled through Sophie's mind. "We've helped others. What is so different this time?" Sophie tried to stay calm and not raise her voice.

"Abba said the new arrival is much like you were in the beginning. He has enjoyed seeing you progress and change. He has asked for my help with this new arrival. I could not refuse."

Pictures of the past few weeks tumbled across Sophie's mind. Of all the sweet times she and Mary shared. Now this news was impossible to accept. She needed her friend Mary more than anyone else ever could. She knew she would always be Mary's favorite no matter how many strays the King brought in. No, this could not happen. Something would have to be done about it. But what? What could she do against those in power? Once they finish with their little clean up experiment, the person can be discarded, passed on to others with the raise of a hand.

Mary laid her hand over her young friends. Sophie yanked away.

"I hoped you would be full of joy knowing another has come out of darkness to join us. Perhaps you might wish to help me for the first few days. Bridget and Darla are always needing another pair of hands, especially the first few hours."

Mary paused, "You and I have rarely spoken of your first days here. Abba asked for me then because he knew you were special and that your needs were greater than most who join us here." Mary looked away, that faraway look Sophie knew so well crossed her friend's face before she continued to speak in a low soft tone, "most do come of their own accord to learn and have fellowship with like-minded people. That was not true of you. And it is not true of the new one I will be helping today."

Sophie looked up at her friend with eyes ready to brim over and let a small smile brighten her countenance. She did not wish to cause Mary more of the pain seen just a moment ago.

CHAPTER 17

Sophie began to tremble recalling the cold, the hunger before the warmth of the large mysterious coach, the warmth seen in the large man's eyes and the lovely lady floating down the curved staircase, followed by the wonderful healing bath where much of her past was discarded. Some of it by magic she did not understand.

The two friends sat quietly, a light mist enveloping them as they each thought their own thoughts.

Sophie gradually let understanding come and listened as Mary continued, "The newest guest is much like you were in the beginning. Abba would not ask for my help with her if he did not feel I was the right person for her at this time and I am pleased to assist in any way that I can."

Sophie looked up again into the beautiful eyes. She loved the face and all of this woman's wise and gentle ways. From her beginning here Sophie knew she stayed because of Mary. But now? She could not hold back the slice of anger. Anger wrapped in fear of rejection caused bile to rise, nearly choking her. But the feeling only lasted for a few moments as a new understanding of the truth of all Mary said calmed her. Things change, unexpected things happen. One must learn to accept change and move on.

Sophie hoped her features revealed nothing of the turmoil she felt. Even with the new understanding, she wasn't ready to openly react. She fought the urge to run from this new reality. "Would you like to help? I know Monika would welcome an extra pair of hands." Mary seemed to relax as she lifted her hand to push back a few loose strands of hair from her forehead.

"Thank you but I believe I will be busy enough with the others." Sophie felt hurt. What else did she feel? Jealousy? Whatever the feeling, she wanted to be left alone for now. She knew she was being selfish, but she needed time to adjust to losing her special time with Mary.

Recalling her plans made in the beginning, Sophie considered. Maybe it was time for her to go, be on her own again but this time she would make better decisions. She was older, healthier, more mature and would be able to make it out in the larger world. She read many books and learned much while here and felt fortified to face things in a different, better way. Perhaps this change could be for the best. Mary would never mean to hurt her but the pain was real. The girl felt a bubble of excitement leak in as she pondered her plan for an adventure outside of the castle.

Mary's voice filtered through the fog, pulling Sophie back, "It is good to be busy. Monika will be able to be with you in a day or two when she finishes the work at hand. She has been out helping those in need, helping families searching for a better life. Monika is good at weaving hope in with food sprinkled with kindness." Mary continued, "Many new ones have come and did not need me, but now and then I am asked for someone special and I am always willing." Mary continued to speak, saying, "One might expect growing pains, and expect hurt feelings even here in Abba's world. Living can be very human, at times most difficult, with suffering found even here."

Sophie listened through feelings of rejection. She wanted to understand. She needed to understand. Rejection here in this place where over time, her guard had dropped, felt nothing like being abandoned out there in the dark world. It was worse!

Outside of the castle walls rejection came and one prepared for it as much as possible, but not here. No, not here. With lowered eyelids, Sophie looked at her friend. Mary continued to sit quietly beside her. Peace settled like a cloak over them. Mary closed her eyes and Sophie thought her friend looked tired and perhaps needed to be somehow refreshed. Maybe Mary should go spend time with Abba. That always seemed to refresh her. Or perhaps take a short holiday. Sophie suggested the idea to Mary.

Mary smiled a wistful smile down at Sophie, extending her hand. "Come and let us go meet the new one before you move to your library tasks or other interests of the day."

Sophie hesitated before taking her friend's hand. As she looked up into the face of her tutor, her mentor, her friend, a grin came softly. Though tears still welled, she let Mary Elizabeth's warmth wrap around her as she prepared to accept the changes that seemed inevitable. With new understanding the young woman made a decision. She would push aside unworthy feelings toward Mary. She loved the woman and owed her a debt that could never be paid.

Sophie felt fortunate to have been brought to Mary in the very beginning. She knew she had been one of the lucky ones. People must be ready and willing to change. Sophie knew she was not the same person who was brought here months ago. But now things were shifting, and she could and probably should make a change in her own life. She would prepare and find the right time to leave and was determined to never make the same mistakes she had made in the past.

Those once trapped in misery could grow strong. Sophie felt certain of that. It takes time and love, but she knew scars healed and love overcomes. Her new strength and things she learned while here would help her to live well once she moved outside again.

Clear hazel eyes searched Mary's face for one long look to be sure. On impulse, Sophie wrapped her arms around the dearest friend ever giving Mary a quick tight hug before stepping away. "Let's go see what the master brought home for you this time."

Mary returned the hug, "Yes, we must go. And I will need to send for Henri."

"Why Henri?"

"Because he is one of the best at so many things in so many ways."

Sophie looked down. "I do not understand. Do you always call him to meet the new ones coming here?"

Mary turned to witness the puzzled look on her young friend's face. She smiled, "No, not always but usually if he is not already busy with someone else and I find he is available. We often ask him for his help doing many different tasks. Why do you ask?"

Sophie wasn't sure.

Waiting a moment before she continued, Mary smiled, "Why do we call on Henri so often when there are many others who could and do serve? The answer is because he is always calm, in good humor and he has an admirable work ethic. He is also very reliable and has a heart for the work we do here. Others will offer and are willing but perhaps do not have the same compassion as our tall friend. We have found Henri has a truly deep empathy for those in need. He has a compartment in his heart full of mercy and truly desires to help when he can."

Mary looked down before she spoke again, "I love Henri. Not more than the others but perhaps in a different way because of his unflinching willingness to help when he can and that is what we all should strive for here with King Abba." Mary paused, "Especially true when we leave the castle in the hopes of helping others."

Understanding filled a void and caused Sophie to gently nod. Soon when the time felt right, she would leave this sanctuary of protection and peace. She would go and try to carry some of the 'Henri" kind of compassion with her. Something she sorely needed and had missed before being brought here months ago. Sophie could have laughed out loud…

CHAPTER 18

Henri Cable waited, resting his tall frame against the iron gate as he watched for his friend Max, (Maximillian Reening), Over time the two melded into the best of friends. Henri lived here in Abba's world by choice embracing all he found here. The outside world held no attraction for Henri. He came many months ago to the castle on his own and alone. The struggle to get here was certainly most difficult through those early days and it took many months. Henri smiled as he remembered the hardships and felt blessed beyond measure once he found the iron gate and entered Abba's world.

Here he found who he was meant to be and what he was meant to do with his life. His mother used to speak with confidence when she spoke of his future.

"Go to the nearest castle and ask for work. While there, seek wisdom and understanding." Henri understood little of what she spoke at the time.

"Once you find the right place, I hope you can and will do what you are good at. You are gifted and should use those gifts to bless others whenever and however you can." Henri was not sure about believing all his mother spoke over him those days so long ago, but her Irish lilt still rang clear in his memory.

When he knew the time was right Henri followed her advice and counsel. Often thought of by others as a solemn man who enjoyed a quiet disciplined life, Henri said he felt blessed beyond measure but wondered if anyone other than Abba understood. His search began when his mother left him. He missed her still.

Henri kicked a pebble and watched it roll away as he continued to wait for Max, recalling again the morning he was found at the iron gate. Abba gave him the life he continued to enjoy today. Three people came to the gate that day and led him to Abba who gently guided him into a new life. All things seemed new from Henri's very first day.

Born and raised to the age of twelve in the hills far to the south, Henri possessed a full measure of common sense along with adequate survival skills. With no father in the home, his mother instructed the young man to leave when she could no longer be with him and to reach the nearest castle. To learn all he could from the one called Abba.

"Go find the right castle and become who you are meant to be." She always added 'once you've learned, give away as much as possible and live a rich full life'. Her words were imprinted on Henri's heart.

The path to this safe haven proved full of many twists and turns until finally he found himself slumped at the iron gate. The peace Henri felt in the rolling hills and gardens of his new home took some getting used to in the beginning. The area was so vast with so much new to learn and appreciate every day and the best part, there was nothing to fear. No hunger or thirst inside the gate. There seemed to be no lack and the people here were different. They offered a kindness he had not encountered outside of the gate.

Many small groups of friends went out from time to time with food, herbs, and hope. Henri soon joined them and enjoyed the trips outside of the castle helping others and he chose to go as often as he could. Now and then he would spend time in other nearby castles, sharing news but the joy of returning to his home never failed to fill him with a joy he found difficult to express even to himself. Yes, Abba's castle was home.

One of the best parts of Henri's world was his friendship with Max. Two more unlikely and different men might be hard to find. One tall and fair, the other of medium height with dark curls falling over his forehead and dimples to take the ladies breath away when he caught their eye with a smile. And that wink! Perhaps the two men understood each other and reveled in their very differences.

Henri usually felt a warm smile coming when he watched Max works his charm on some defenseless female. Henri felt sure Max meant no harm and he easily forgave him because the rascal made him laugh when others could not.

As close as the two were Henri felt a stab of worry now and again, more a warning really. At odd times Max spoke in off color ways making Henri uncomfortable. Totally wrong as far as Henri was concerned. When this happened, Henri tried to shrug it off as a poor joke not to be repeated, readily forgiving Max, thinking he needed to have more faith in his friend. Henri simply enjoyed his friend too much to reprimand him. He would not let himself dwell on his handsome friends' errant ways. At least most of the time.

Henri was over six feet tall when not slumped forward to hear someone speak or bending his sand-colored head of hair over a task. Sophie liked his looks but would not have called him handsome. Pleasantly plain came to mind. Some Of the others spoke of their admiration for the young man who always seemed calm and pleasant with a direct way of looking at you when he spoke to you.

Sophie noticed one outstanding feature. Henri's long eyelashes swept his cheeks when his eyes were closed. As thin as a willow with the bluest of eyes that were so penetrating at times, she was forced to look away to avoid his seeing into her soul.

Henri only smiled if anyone mentioned his being different and the peculiar way people analyzed him, usually ones who barely knew him.

Henri only let himself grin an 'oh, whatever' kind of smirk when Max mentioned such nonsense to him. It usually came with a comical twinkle in his friend's eye. Ridiculous and not worth discussing.

Henri could not stop people from thinking and he did have a sliver of something he and his mother shared. Ah, how he missed her still. Many years since the sickness came ripping her from their hearth and turning his world upside down. She prepared him with all she had within her, instructing and encouraging him to live a worthwhile life. He would honor his mother's wishes as long as he lived.

Henri waited and watched Max saunter toward him, late as usual. The two spent time bending over the list of their tasks for the day. It was simply their way of getting a similar mindset for the work ahead.

The friends enjoyed being together for another day, an obvious fact to those around them.

"We have to maintain our reputation for being good at everything, cannot let folks see how false that might be." Henri chuckled and stretched out his long strides forcing Max to jog.

A groan from Max, "Do we have to? How about we save some of our most excellent work for another time."

Henri almost smiled, familiar with Max and his groans as though he was being asked to jump into a pit of snakes or be prepared to die for some unworthy cause. In truth, Max cheerfully came alongside once Henri led the way.

CHAPTER 19

Three or four times a year Henri and Max were asked to plan a longer trip and venture to outlying castles and distant seaports to bring back reports of needs. Others would be sent out later to help those in the report. The system worked and help was given where needed. Max filled with excitement when Henri gave him a certain look, "We probably could finish early today and tramp out this afternoon to see old friends. Perhaps take supplies enough for a longer trip soon, maybe be out for a few days."

Max lit up, his eyebrows lifted up and down in a comical way, "sounds like a solid idea to me. A little 'super special' work to keep our skills honed. When do we leave?"

"Don't get too excited yet. Today will be a day trip. But we'll make a plan soon?"

Max appreciated his friend's ability to carefully plan each trip out. Being prepared with enough food, water and other basics Max left to Henri. Being organized and prepared are things Max didn't do well.

"Where to 'Oh fine', leader once we finish here?" Max expressed more than once having no need to lead, he would laugh, "If trouble comes, just carry on. I promise to catch up."

Henri did not take offense. The slender young man did not believe Max meant to use his friend's, it was just the way Max sorted things out. Or so Henri chose to believe. The affection between the two was mutual and the arrangement developed over time worked for both.

Henri smiled as Max chattered on and his excitement grew. Max always called their short trips on the outside of the castle Abba's 'comity' work.

The trips seemed to be more frequent lately and Henri noticed a definite change in his friend after their most recent journey. He hoped nothing stirred to draw Max away, back into the dark. Not all trips were in safe areas where most of the citizens enjoyed peace and a bit of prosperity. At times teams traveled darker paths taking food and medicine to those who were in need but did not know how to ask for help.

Unwelcome changes in Max were more noticeable to Henri on their last trip once their work was finished and they returned from spending time with folks in some darker areas. Henri tried to brush aside the concern that clawed at his thoughts. He hoped he misread his friend and was wrong. But still the sliver of worry hung around like a small swarm of gnats.

The two young men finished the day's lists of small tasks early and prepared to spend the rest of the day outside of the castle. They should be back by nightfall.

As the two friends tramped the trail leading across a grove of birch trees, Henri felt joy in Max. They spoke of things learned concerning self-discipline, Henri doing his usual, getting his thoughts across in a few words. Henri loved his life and his soft words revealed it to any who was near and would hear. Max always seemed to listen. Henri explained, "We will deliver supplies and a bit of hope to those we find, then return to the castle before nightfall."

The warm memories of baskets of fruit and fresh vegetables left on their stoop when his mother became most ill stayed with the young man. Perhaps that is why Henri loved being outside, working in the orchards and vegetable patches so much. The castle shared their abundance, a work of gift giving Henri loved. Perhaps that being the best part - seeing the faces when a basket full of fresh food was given, along with a kind word and a smile.

Henri knew some of the folks they visited but often left a basket on a stoop. No 'thank you' was needed. Henri loved all of it and he longed for Max to feel the same. Max had a cheerful way about him when they worked outside, in the gardens, but he did not help with the new ones brought in from the dark, some in wretched condition. Max left that works to Henri and the others.

Henri, on the other hand, loved everything offered in this good life and when asked, he cheerfully accepted any challenge, especially when a new one needed help and Mary called on him to work through the first difficult hours. Yes, Henri loved his life, wore his quiet joy as a soft cloak. Large enough to wrap around anyone who came near with a need.

"Where are we off to today my lean leader? What good works do you have lined up for us?" Max grinned and lifted his brow in a comical way a couple of times before leading off at a trot ahead of Henri.

Henri shook his head, "Just follow me as usual and we will be fine."

Max laughed as he slowed his pace, "I will be a good follower." The two returned home before dark with Max growing quiet when they reached the castle.

The following morning the two met again and once again planned to go out of the castle for the day. Max could not hide his pleasure from his friend. Henri said Abba requested another day trip without giving a reason. They would be leaving soon but first Mary needed his help.

Max tapped his foot at the delay. He was anxious to get away from the castle and hated being kept later than he'd hoped today but Henri would not leave until he helped Mary with Abba's newest arrival. Henri always said, 'it won't take long' but it always took longer than Max wanted, leaving him grunting in frustration. Still, it really turned out to be a short delay. Just long enough for Henri and three other friends to carry the needed hot water for Mary. Then the two friends prepared to be out for the rest of the day.

CHAPTER 20

When Mary Elizabeth and Sophie reached the area, the hot water was being delivered and when the tub was full of steaming water, Henri and the other helpers left to plan the rest of their day. Mary spoke briefly to Abba before being joined by Monika and Darla. Darla appeared paler than usual. Everyone was aware the girl was ill or troubled, but she didn't ask for help or offer any reason.

Nodding to Mary, Henri said while leaving, "We've carried the hot water to the room we used last, so we will leave you ladies to do your good work. Max and I are off to visit some folks."

Henri reached Max, "We are now finished here so let us be off."

Max smiled, "Sounds good." The two walked back to the side gate, gathered up their backpacks of supplies for the day and set off into the woods at a steady pace.

In the same hour Sophie watched the process of healing and renewal for the one now being cared for. She looked on from a distance. Someone she recognized as a friend of Henri's came and, when directed by Mary, carried the bundle of refuse to the room full of steam. Sophie smiled knowing Henri instructed the water brought in to be as hot as possible for the tub. The bundle tried to move. Sophie watched from a safe distance and every emotion in her quaked and spilled out as tears of understanding and compassion swept over her.

How can Mary go through this again and again? Sophie stayed back in the alcove, knowing she could not help, only watch. Her tears slid down her cheeks and soaked the front of her bodice. Standing in the shadow Sophie watched the now familiar routine unfold, in much the same way as it did the night of her arrival. Sophie hoped the soul hidden under the rags would survive and even thrive.

Mary Elizabeth thanked the ladies who came to help before the careful work of restoration began. Sophie continued to silently weep in the shadows.

Once outside of the castle, Henri focused on his list while Max tried to control his excitement at being once again out in the world. "We have only three stops we must make, then we will venture to find if there are others we might see and perhaps encourage while we are out." Henri tried to ignore the swell of excitement Max exhibited. He would try to keep Max focused and get back to the Castle before dark.

"We are going further today, is that right? To areas we have not visited before, right?" Henri wondered what notions were going on behind the sparkle of excitement in the eyes of his friend. Henri hid his concern behind his solemn expression.

"Will we be able to travel as far as the sea today?"

Henry, surprised by the questions, said, "No, not this trip. I believe we will plan the longer trip soon. Is that something you would like to do? Go to the seashore again?"

Max gave Henri a sidelong look, unsure, "I would love to see the ships again and smell the sea salt, talk to some of the men back from the deep and listen to their stories of strange lands. Is that something you desire also?"

Henri smiled a small smile, hoping to reassure his friend, "That sounds to be a good three maybe a four-day trip out. But we will plan such a trip and soon. There are always some in need everywhere these days."

Max grinned his agreement, "Yes, it would have to be a longer trip out to be sure. We could see a new bit of country." Max paused, lifting his eyes. The glint of longing in his friend's eyes wasn't missed by Henri.

Lifting his chin, Max said, “A longer trip would give us a sense of the needs of some who are further from the castle.”

Henri actually chuckled, “It would be good to take a broader look at ways we might help. Good of you to think about those we so far have not reached.”

Max quickly agreed, “You make the plans, and I will be right there with you!”

The few stops on their list were quickly dispatched, blessing families with a promise to come again soon before the two friends turned back toward the castle. Max grew quite, the sparkle in his eyes once again gone as they reached the iron gate.

Henri noticed and wondered what he could do and how much he could promise in order to fill the emptiness lately found in his friend. He decided he would go speak with Abba soon, perhaps find a way to help his friend find the peace that he himself enjoyed. Henri let silence cover him as they walked. This restlessness in Max was unlike Darla's problem. Her bouts of melancholia and sadness came from some loss she refused to speak of. Mary once remarked it must be something deeply personal. Mary felt and understood these things better than most.

Later the same week Henri sought out Sophie one evening as she rested alone on a bench in the garden, Autumn colors scattered about in all directions.

“Mind some company? I do not wish to intrude.”

Sophie, pleasantly surprised, said, “Of course not. Please join me.” She felt secretly pleased by his presence. They sat for several minutes, not speaking before Sophie looked at her friend, “Is something wrong? You seem your quiet self but I feel you are concerned. Some vexing problem perhaps.”

Henri looked at her as though seeing her for the first time, “Be careful or folks will be saying you have knowing ways much like Mary.”

Sophie laughed, “They already say that about you, don't they?”

She remembered both Mary and Max at different times speaking of things Henri knew that he could not know. Henri in his way and Mary, with understanding beyond her years, both speaking with wisdom to help sort out something troubling a friend. Henri brought his calm balance and without knowing how or caring why, he blessed others.

Each would leave this solemn young man feeling better, often with a changed perspective and more hope.

Sophie shifted to see the contour of his face more clearly, "Do you want to tell me about it?"

Henri again looked at her as though seeing her for the first time, "You know my friend Max. I feel a change in him and am at a loss as to how to help him if indeed he needs my help."

Sophie became thoughtful. "I do not know his story. Max, I mean. But I remember clearly my first day and the first few days that followed. It might be his inability to believe he can have all that is offered here because he still clings to small pieces of himself left out in the dark. Perhaps he perceives loss when there is none. Nothing he has lost is worth going back out into the dark to get. But Max must learn that for himself."

Henri stood, "Thank you. I've enjoyed your insight. I guess I shall wait and see and hope for the best of outcomes." Sophie stood to say goodbye to her troubled friend.

CHAPTER 21

Early one cool morning while in the garden, Sophie realized she was starting her seventh month at the castle. The days passed with purpose, so many tasks and projects to work on caused days to become weeks. Without her little daily lists, she might be lost. Her favorite times were her hours in the library, dusting and checking books for damage, replacing, cataloging, all of her hours spent there were true joy. And she read. Books were a special medicine for her, giving her a glimpse of the vast world around her.

Still, the old feeling of wanting to go again to the seashore swept in and she began to make plans. *I will go alone. I am sure I shall be fine.* Now that much of Mary's time kept her busy with others and the weather still held warm, Sophie knew the days of pleasant mild weather would not hold off the coming cold winter for long. She would go, leave just for a day, maybe two.

"The plan is a good one. It will be a test of sorts." Sophie spoke to herself, feeling confident. A small bubble of fear might be expected. Sophie, no longer a child felt strong and capable of being on her own, at least for a few hours.

The plan finally in place, Sophie decided to leave early the following morning. She checked to be sure she would not be needed for anything pressing for the next few days. She would take enough supplies for three days away from the castle although she expected to be back in one, perhaps no more than two days.

Her heart pounded in her chest as she thought of once again seeing the village and the shoreline where she spent her last wretched night outside of the castle. She would be back before dark her first day out alone if all went well. *I truly do not want to cause worry.*

Remembering recent outside excursions, Sophie smiled. She and Mary delivered a baby once, a beautiful little girl. The joy and the fulfillment overwhelmed her. To help in small ways to make lives easier blessed her as nothing else could.

A few months ago, she was consumed by her own selfish needs and wants. Her desire for wealth and comfort! Sophie laughed. She now enjoyed a new kind of wealth and comfort. But even so, she would be bold and journey out for a day.

Early the following morning Sophie gathered her pack of supplies and slipped out of the garden through the side gate. She did feel an odd restlessness, perhaps from spending less time with Mary the past few days.

Sophie thought of those who left and never returned. She felt an emptiness at the thought. Well, she would go, get the feeling of being in control of her new destiny and speak to Mary in a day or so. Mary often spoke of free will and the ability to use it anyway one might choose. A gift to be used wisely. Hooray for free will! It felt wonderful to have her very own secret, to go out alone, away from her protectors. Her friends.

Walking away in the early morning mist, Sophie felt her chest swell with confidence and excitement. Still, perhaps she should have mentioned her plan to Mary, or to someone. She meant no harm, so why this gentle press of doubt? Or fear, whatever name one might give to this new feeling, she wanted to be rid of it and enjoy the day. Sophie walked into the woods, along familiar paths. The quiet morning gave Sophie time to sort out her thoughts.

Hours passed quickly, the sun slipped low in the west before she took notice and felt a chill. How far had she walked? Realizing it too late to make it back to the castle in time for the lamps to be doused, she searched for a safe place to rest. Already a mistake for a one-day trip!

Ashamed of her foolishness, Sophie determined to spend the night out and pay more attention to the time tomorrow. She soon found a grove of slender willow trees and tall ferns where she could hide, wrap in her heavy cloak and sleep a few hours before returning home.

Fragmented glimpses of her grim past pushed up into her consciousness. It was not her first night alone in the dark. But this time was different. This time she felt prepared. The knowledge she belonged, with a new family and friends to protect and even love her unconditionally gave her strength. Yes, she would start back at first light in the morning.

Once wrapped and sheltered for sleep, Sophie felt vulnerable, all but forgotten memories filtered in with unnerving clarity. Was it from being away from Mary and the others? The pictures were so wrenching, forcing tears to fall. Slowly her thinking cleared. *Why would anyone for any reason move back into the past heartbreak once they were rescued and safe!*

Taking a deep breath, Sophie felt her muscles relax and a warm blanket of peace covered her. She slept until something pulled her from sleep. Something that did not belong. Sophie slowly sat up.

An out-of-place sound startled her awake. She listened and waited as the sound of footfalls could still be heard. Someone passed nearby but she could see nothing in the dark through the grove of slender birch and willow trees. She barely let out breath until the steps faded and the night quiet fell once more but the few minutes of fear brought bile to her throat. Sophie realized she needed more time with Mary and the others in the castle before confronting strangers on the outside, especially at night. Filling her mind with the image of Mary and the other friends at the castle she again felt protected and safe in her resting place and lay down to sleep until dawn.

The morning sun washed over the swaddled girl pulling her from sleep. She searched in her pack for a biscuit and wondered how far she might be from the coast. Could she dare take another day? She would be missed by some and alarms would be sounded. She chastised herself again for not leaving a note or speaking to someone. The last thing she wanted was to cause unnecessary concern.

Still, now that she could be close to the sea, she stood and shook out her robe, gathered her satchel and decided to strike out for the bay. The village should be close, and she would love to walk the cobblestones as a healthy, normal, person. She would spend an hour at the most along the shoreline then hurry home. Yes, she could smell the salt air and still be back before dark. She wanted to see that village through her new eyes.

Sophie smiled at the thought of reaching the sea. She reminded herself that she was free to go and to do anything she wished. The plan seemed reasonable, and she felt sure the last village she remembered should not be far. How long had the ride with Abba taken? She slept on part of the ride, but it must not have been a long ride to the castle that night, so she felt confident. Thinking it over, the plan seemed reasonable, with just a small niggle of doubt. If she did not find the village by mid-day, she would turn for home.

CHAPTER 22

Shouts echoed through the hallway of the castle. Mary Elizabeth wondered at the commotion, not all that unusual but this clatter seemed different, louder. She headed toward the sound that seemed to be coming from one of the sunrooms. Moving swiftly toward the problem Monika bumped into Mary jogging in the same direction.

"What is the problem?" Mary kept pace with her young friend.

Mary and Monika reached Henri who arrived just ahead of them, "Max is gone. It appears he left sometime yesterday."

"Some of his favorite things are missing." True sorrow could be heard in Henri's voice. Other friends were chiming in with their thoughts.

Mary witnessed the pain in Henri's eyes, "Who sounded the alarm? After all he has the right to leave, to go, this is not a prison. You must not condemn yourself, Henri. Not everyone wants what we have here. No one can be blamed."

Henri stopped suddenly, "How can you always be so calm? Maybe you do not form lasting attachments," Henri blurted out, then stopped and straightened, "Sorry." The moment passed. "but I do blame myself. You see, I noticed small things. He spoke in ways that worried me, but I didn't want to press Max, so I did nothing. I should have found some way to help him adjust. Been a better friend."

Henri stretched his tall frame, "I felt his restlessness and tried to compensate in my own way with my own contentment. I always tried to find things to do more to his liking. He never seemed to find himself, his true self. I failed my friend." Henri slumped on a nearby bench.

"Nonsense," Mary placed her hand on Henri's shoulder, "Some come, stay awhile and decide for whatever reason to leave. Again, I remind you, this is a safe peaceful place, not some prison," Mary looked away before looking again at her young friend, "What if it were you who left?" She looked off into space for a moment, "What would you expect me and the others who care about you to do?"

Henri lifted his head, a new light in his eyes, "Of course…." his voice trailed off as another friend came rushing in, her voice raised. "Sophie is gone! Some of her things, her heavy cloak, oh, I do not know what all. She is missing! Her water skin she takes when we go out, it is gone!" the girl shook from head to toe, "I tell you she has left!"

This news brought shock and a sense of loss to both Mary and Henri.

Turning, Mary asked, "When did you last see her? Have you been with her, Monika?"

"I guess I haven't seen her since we worked together in the library. Two days ago, I think." Seeing the troubled expressions around her, Monika looked up at Henri. "You look terrible."

Mary smiled, in spite of the situation they were facing, "You do have a way with words! It seems Max and Sophie have both left us. No one seems sure exactly when."

A question spilled from the small woman," Did they leave together?"

"No, we have no reason to think so, Max may have left earlier."

Mary looked at Henri, arching her brows, "You were about to say we need a plan. A plan to go find our two friends and see if they are safe and happy. If they both choose to remain out, we must accept their right to do so."

"Yes, that is exactly what we must do. We will find them, make sure they are safe, help them if they need us." Henri looked at Mary, "What shall we do first?" The determination in the young man's eyes could not be missed. He would implement and follow the plan once everyone felt ready.

Mary tipped her head sideways, "You are right. Both of our friends have been gone for a few hours. Not long. We need a few searchers. Any volunteers?"

Monika spoke first, "Me and Darla will gather needed supplies for the trip. I will talk to Bridget so she can cover things for the three of us until Darla and I return."

Quiet for a moment, Monika said, "It will be good for Darla to be out in the countryside away from the castle for a good stretch of the legs." She smiled her quirky grin, "We will make sure she knows she is needed. I'll enlist her help because we do need her and I think it will cheer her. She has been very sad of late. Perhaps this will be the medicine she needs."

Mary's expression held compassion. "We do not need to know everything, and Darla is a joy to be around much of the time. I trust she will resolve whatever is troubling her in her own way."

"You are right. I do believe it will be a good thing to get her outside of the castle. See some new places." Monika turned to go find and talk with Darla.

Mary nodded her understanding, "I agree and a good outcome will be to find our friends."

Henri stepped closer, feeling more positive, "I know much of the country around, all the way to the sea and some of the villages along the shore."

Mary turned to leave, "Good, but first we will meet with Abba. He knows where both Sophie and Maximillian were found. I believe he told me once they were found in two different villages not too distant from each other."

The small group followed Mary to seek needed advice and instruction from the king. Their spirits were full of a new determination and hope. Mary Elizabeth always knew where to begin. Each of the friends started making mental lists of what might be needed and within the hour the group of four friends were ready. They set off in search of Max and Sophie, with Abba's instructions tucked in their hearts.

CHAPTER 23

Rain threatened but the morning skies remained clear as the small group struck off at a good pace and traveled across meadows and wooded areas, with Henri revealing a shortcut from time to time along the way to save time in reaching the seashore. They rested for a noon meal of biscuits and cheese before continuing west. They knew of two villages where they might find their friends but probably not together. Getting weary as dusk fell, the group pushed on into the falling darkness.

"Do you think they will come to harm in the night?" Darla spoke more to herself than to the others.

Monika heard and stopped Darla to tighten her friend's scarf, "We will find them before any real harm comes. Try to be confident."

Darla nodded, "I will. I just think these two have so much to give. In different ways, of course. To lose either of them would break my heart."

Mary heard and agreed, "It would be difficult for many of us. But we must not fear. First, we will find them, see if they need us. One step at a time." Her voice was calm, comforting.

The beautiful Mary and somber Henri moved through the darkness, guided only by the vague light of the rising moon and early starlight in the north.

Trusting the stars for direction, Mary and Henri knew many of the constellations. They also knew they were covered in hope by those who were left behind at the castle. Stopping to check their bearings from time to time, Mary felt no fear for her own safety, only for Sophie. And for Max. Ah, Max, who always left a little dust of worry, and always with a twinkle in his eyes and tap, tap of his feet. Mary knew he was priceless.

Thinking of Sophie as a new one to the castle, Mary's lips curled in a soft smile. She pondered how long each one coming in for a better life should be considered 'new'.

Mary felt a fondness for Sophie from the very beginning, from her first reveal under all the hurt and filth inflicted on the girl. So much beauty came after her first few hours. Mary remembered the draw of wanting to protect the lovely hazel eyed girl from their earliest days together.

Mary knew Henri felt the same for Max. The small group would do all they could to help these two loved ones. If and when they found them!

As they traveled toward the sea, Mary let memories of her own first days of being safe and clean and warm and well-fed flow through her. The self-hate and self-pity slowly washed away one patch at a time being replaced by all things good. *How is it possible that such restoration of the human soul can and does take place?* Perhaps when one is safe and free there is space to heal, to change, to accept, to grow in wisdom and understanding.

The group kept to a steady pace. The small force of four pushed on strong and determined without complaint.

"I think I smell the salt in the mist." As Henri spoke, Darla cried "I see lights. A village is just there, see the lights?"

Mary said, "Perhaps we should separate into teams. Darla and I could stay and search this village and, Henri, you and Monika could go up the shoreline to the next village. We will search here and whatever happens, we will follow you in three hours or less."

Henri liked the plan. He and Monika turned with a wave.

"See you soon and we will pray for success."

After separating, Mary and Darla moved toward the circle of lights seen shrouded in mist, both feeling the excitement of finding a village. Hoping. Could this be the right village? They would soon know.

The two women heard a clock strike in a nearby tower as they moved down the first street they came to. The hour grew late.

In a village farther east along the shoreline from where they left Mary and Darla, Monika pointed, "Are those lights?"

Henri held his hand above his brow to shade his eyes, "Yes, I see the lights. Let's hope it is the place we are looking for." Less than half an hour later the two friends entered the village. They could clearly see the flickering street lamps strung in the distance and soon stood under one in the vague circle of light falling on the cobblestones.

Monika stopped, "I need a short rest before we go on. Just a few moments while we decide where to start our search." Looking up at Henri, "do you have any idea of how or where to look?"

Henri stopped to lean against one of the tall lampposts.

"We will do all we can do and trust it will be enough."

A few minutes of rest before beginning their search in earnest for their friend could do no harm…

CHAPTER 24

Earlier, a few miles west of where Henri and Monika rested, Mary and Darla stood in a similar vague circle of light.

Darla sighed. Mary noticed and said, "We will take a short rest and consider before we venture further. Get our footing so to speak."

Darla whispered, "Thank you." The weary woman moved to lean against a building and sliding down, settled to the ground.

Mary moved a few paces away and stood under the eve of a stone structure. She waited in the silence surrounding her while her eyes adjusted to every light and shadow around them.

Mary focused on the shadows in the lanes and could see down the row of lamp posts flickering to guide those out past dusk. Some distance from where she stood, she watched as someone slowly moved into view. The person could barely be seen at this distance.

Mary's heart lurched inside of her. *Could it be? There seemed something familiar in the person's movements. Could it really be this easy? All one had to do - is be determined, seek out a trail to follow and never waiver in your faith of the right of your cause? Never quit because of weariness or cold or the dark, the unknown? Could being determined be enough?*

Go, find the little one who might still lack understanding? All babes start off on milk. It takes time and nurturing to build the strength needed to hold fast to a new, safe life. Mary understood that in the past Sophie trusted others many times, only to be disappointed, even harmed.

"Come, Darla, let's go see what's under yonder light." She chuckled as she took Darla's hand, helping her friend up and leading the way.

Sophie, standing under the lamppost watched the two come toward her, and called out, "Well, hello there. What are you two doing so far from your beds on such a foggy night as this?"

Even with a grin across her face, she looked puzzled for a moment before running to hug her friends, Mary first.

"Might not be the night to be wandering about. Looks like rain could be coming." What could one do but laugh? Sophie seemed fine, perfectly fine.

Mary joked, "We did not want you to get cold or lonely out in the night all by yourself."

Darla stood back, trying to make up her mind whether to be truly angry or be overcome with relief. The latter won. She hugged her friend, as a thought flashed, *how different now from the wretch brought into the castle only a few months ago.*

"Maybe you will be kind enough to let us head for home now." Sophie reached for Darla's hand. Darla almost smiled but not all the way to her eyes and the realization settled over Sophie. She became somber knowing she caused her friends worry and a hard day's march to come out into the damp night to find her. Her head down, chin almost touching her chest, "I am a contemptible friend. I should have told someone." Looking into Mary's eye's, "I meant to return the first day before being missed but I lost track of time and longed to smell the sea once more before returning. So selfish, I am sorry, I planned to be out for only a few hours…"

Mary wrapped her arms around both Darla and Sophie, "As long as you are safe and no harm has come to any of us, all is well." She paused, remembering the others, "But Henri and Monika have gone ahead to the next village in hopes of finding Max. We need to go now before it gets any later. They may need our help."

Sophie did not move, "Max is missing?" Sophie felt the weight of cold fear for Henri's friend.

"Yes, he must have left before you decided to trek off on your own. Or perhaps near the same hour." Mary's voice remained soft and calm. No condemnation or anger was heard. "We believe he, too, has been gone less than two full days."

The three turned north-east along the bay. They believed the next village just a few miles further up the shoreline. Though growing weary, the small group of three felt an urgency to find and rejoin Henri and Monika as soon as possible. The hour grew even later and the skies felt menacing.

They found the village without difficulty, weary but excited. And they soon found the only two people out at such a late hour. Two familiar people!

"Henri and Monika, thankful we are to find you quickly and safe."

Henri looked past Mary and frowned as he caught Sophie's gaze, "Well, I see one of the lost is found." His dear face was expressionless except for his eyes. Sophie knew he was unhappy with her but surely, he must be a little happy to see her. She just knew it! And it pleased her to see him, even under these circumstances.

Mary stepped between the two, "Any news of Max?" Mary looked away, her hand shielding her eyes, but only vague lamp lights were visible in the mist.

"We only passed a couple of people, the hour being so late, and…" Just then Henri straightened. Something moved, caught the corner of his eye. He pointed down the narrow avenue and raised his hand to his brow. All five friends looked in the direction Henri pointed. Someone or something moved into the lamplight.

Sophie said, "I followed someone today. I believe they passed where I rested in the night, but I stopped thinking about the incident when I reached places familiar."

Mary turned, "We must go see. Whoever it is may need our help at this late hour."

Henri spoke, angry, "Just a moment! Before we do anything, Miss Sophie, could you please tell us what you were doing out here alone?"

Sophie almost laughed before speaking, "Oh, Henri, I wanted to see if I could be safe out alone for a few hours and night fell before I expected. As I said, someone passed during the night but did not see me and passed on. I traveled quite far from the castle before stopping to rest, so I decided to be gone a bit longer and smell the salty sea before heading home." Sophie paused, "There was a moment when I thought to follow and see who passed me in the night but felt a warning, so I just curled up and slept until dawn." She stopped to take a breath and looked at Henri, "I always planned to return tonight." She tried to feel remorse for the worry caused but felt such joy in seeing her friends, especially Henri, she just scrunched her face, trying not to smile.

Henry and Mary both spoke at the same time, "You could have been hurt or even killed!" Henri, never jovial, was obviously angry with Sophie.

In her own defense, she said, "At the time I thought it might be someone from the castle. But I discarded that idea and the time flew by and I slept."

"Obviously!" Henri raised his voice even more. Sophie did not know if he felt relieved or still angry or what?

She snapped, "I was returning to the castle when I recognized Mary and Darla coming toward me." Her voice softened, "I could not believe what I saw. It was wonderful to have companions to travel back home with."

Sophie turned to smile at her friends, "Once again I am sorry it grew so late before I noticed the hour. The days are so much shorter now that winter is growing closer, and darkness falls quickly."

Everyone could feel Henri's suppressed anger. "What foolishness. You should be watched for your own protection! At the very least, someone needs to instruct you in the telling of time by the stars."

The good, usually soft-spoken young man continued to grumble and mutter under his breath. Mary, her eyes still focused down the way, stepped in to stop emotions from getting out of control, "We need to find Max."

As Mary pointed, all eyes turned toward the lamppost in the distance. The same one Henri pointed to earlier. "I want to see who or what is there," Mary started toward the light some distance away at the end of the lane.

The small band walked toward the lamppost where a crumpled mound slumped in the vague light. Henri taking long strides reached the lamppost first.

Squatting down to lift the scrap of worn burlap, Henri looked into the eyes of his friend Max. Max whispered, "It's you. I believed." His voice barely heard, cracked.

Shocked, Henri breathed a prayer of thanks for finding his friend. Max was in worse condition than expected but otherwise safe.

Max looked up at his friend, his eyes brimming, ready to overflow. "Ah, Henri I knew you would come." His hand reached to touch his friend's arm. "I told Benjamin you would come." Max wiped a tear from his dirt-stained cheek.

Henri gave Max a drink of water from his waterskin.

"To say I am sorry is sad but true. I thought I wanted more excitement, thought I was missing out on broader things offered in life, but I was wrong. I thought I would find old friends, only to find they were not friends, never had been." Tears continued to leak down the young man's bruised face, "It is a dark, cruel world out here, isn't it Henri?"

Henri could see Max had survived a beating, perhaps several beatings and only two days passed since he left the castle! Henri pulled his friend to his feet, "Yes it can be cruel. You have been hurt but are still alive. For that we are so grateful."

Henri's arms wrapped around Max, "And the good news is we are all safe now and can go back. There will be others needing our help." Henri held his friend, pushing off the rags with one hand and reached to toss his wild curly hair with the other, "We are a team remember? Let's go home."

Max jerked away, unable to forget so quickly the wrongs, "They beat me. And Benjamin, they beat him, too and without cause, taking everything, even our shoes. They took those last when we were all but dead." Henri comforted his friend then asked, "Who is this Benjamin you speak of? Where is he now."

Sophie looked down at the battered man's feet. "His boots really are gone." Sophie noticed his feet were crusted and surely cold. She removed her long scarf as Monika did the same. They bent down and wrapped his feet one at a time while Mary and Henri supported their friend. How could so much destruction happen in such a short period of time? They would wait for answers.

"They were once my friends," Max stuttered, "at least, I believed they were." Henri gave Max another drink of water from his waterskin as Max continued, "Henri, they took my cloak and coat, my coin. I tried to tell them. I wanted to tell them…"

"Don't try to talk. We are together now, and you are safe."

Henri wrapped his long coat around his friend.

Mary saw Max stiffen, "Wait, we need to help Benjamin. He has suffered much more than I. He is just over there, I think. By the corner of that building." He pointed. "I think that is where he gave me this piece of blanket. He shared what little he had. We need to find him." Max called out, "Ben, where are you?"

Henri shielded his eyes and noticed a shadow by a small cluster of saplings near a small shack. "I think there is something in those shadows. Just there." Pointing, Henri let Sophie take Max's arm and he jogged over to the shadows. He found a heap of humanity and bent to uncover the face beneath. "Bring more water and dried fruit or a biscuit if you have any left."

The band of friends rushed to where Henri stood in the shadows. They formed a circle around the newly found soul. After drinking a little water and eating a bit of fruit the young man's vision seemed to clear. He saw Max. "Ah, my friend I see they did come for you." His voice cracked, "Those are the sort of friends one truly needs. "

Max, with his strength quickly returning, said, "Yes, Benjamin, they came and now we are all here together. Will you come with us?" Touching his friend's arm, "I cannot leave you here."

Henri turned to look into the eyes of his friend, "Are you sure, Max? He will need a true friend in the months to come."

Max, still weak, winked, "I am ready and, I am sure." Still suffering from the beating he had taken, Max leaned on Sophie and held out his hand to help his new friend to his feet.

A harsh sob pierced the air. All eyes turned toward the sound to see Darla, standing just behind Monika, trying to breathe. Catching her breath, the disbelief on her face quickly changed to joy, something never before seen by her friends.

"Benny, is it really you? Can it be true after all these months?" The always quiet, reserved Darla glowed with an aura of joy, the constant deep sadness gone from her features. Amazing!

"Do you know Benjamin?" Mary spoke first, her voice soft, filled with wonder. Darla turned to Mary, her face soaked with tears still holding Benjamin's hand, her voice cracking, "He is my brother." Darla turned to Max, "Thank you for finding my brother." Darla smiled as the tears continued to flow down to her chin.

Max seemed humbled by her words, "In truth it was more Ben finding me. He tried to help me but couldn't, just too long without food or water and his beatings must have been far worse." Turning to Henri, "we will help him, won't we?"

With a direct knowing look, Henri said, "Truer words were never spoken. Indeed, we will do all we can for this one."

Max, bruised and filthy, could still smile and wink. More dried fruit and meat and water refreshed both young men. It would take time for Benjamin to recover but Darla, along with the others, would see to it that all his needs were met. At least as long as he would let them!

Max and Henri steadied Benjamin between them. Henri actually smiled, "Mary, let's go home. If we press, we can be there by sunrise. Just in time for hot tea and biscuits."

Mary laughed, "Or hot soup at the noonday meal. Might be good to rest from time to time. I think we are all tired and there is no need to rush now that the lost are found and safe."

Tired but too excited to rest, the small group of seven pressed north toward the castle. A cold wind blew and increased before dawn as they hiked toward home. They were all tired but elated, still feeling the overflow of emotions, (if elation and exhaustion could be felt at the same time). They kept a slow steady pace toward safety.

Suddenly something changed. In an instant, the wind slacked and turned to a breeze, a warm breeze. Looking up, they noticed a change in the canopy of stars overhead. The light from the full moon in the nearly cloudless sky brightened and changed. The small band of hikers moved closer together, their faces turned as one toward the cone of light shining down on them. For no understandable reason, their faces lit into smiles.

They stood still in the warm circle of light and began to hear sounds, so soft at first, they brought confusion. Mary heard music, a kind of instrumental sound, Henri heard leaves rustling even though most of the trees were quite bare. Sophie thought she heard some bells from far off in the distance. Standing next to Mary, Sophie and Henri both spoke at once, "Yes I hear it but what makes such a sound?'

From somewhere out in the universe the various sounds filtered across the landscape again and again in waves. The sounds began to change, to mingle together on the soft warm breeze that wrapped around the small group. The cone of light still covered them with its unusual presence, "Makes me want to sing." Henri looked up, speaking to no one in particular.

Benjamin, a warm expression evident, began to weep. The toll taken on his body these past months and now surrounded by his sister and new companions, with this strange warmth and comfort filling the marrow in his bones, the exhausted young man sank to the ground. Darla settled down by her brother soaking in the wonder of these moments. Gathered in a ball of humanity, all seven knew they should move but hesitated, not ready to leave this magical circle of moonlight.

Everyone under the cone of light heard the sounds change to a soft moan. All heads turned in one direction as the sounds changed, shifted, coming from behind them then from in front. It filled the air becoming louder. Max spoke to the breeze swirling with the sound all around them, "Please stop." and to the group, he said, "I think we should go now." Pulling Benjamin to his feet, "I just want to get to my bed. We both just want to go home."

Henri smiled, "You are right. One can only stay in a perfect place for a little while." Looking at the others he said, "Are we ready to get home in time for tea?"

As the group of friends moved out of the circle of light surrounding them, they could still hear soft music on the warm breeze...

CHAPTER 25

Reaching from the cocoon of warm blankets, Sophie fumbled for the snooze button on her alarm clock before the music could change to its loud annoying buzz. Once the alarm went to silence, Sophie remained motionless, troubled. *What a long night. All of it so vivid, seemed so real.*

Total silence filled her bedroom as Sophie tried to shake off the images still clinging to places in her mind. They were from a faraway place and from a time long ago. A world that filled her night, (a dream perhaps - she felt unsure). In a few minutes, she must start this new day.

The young wife snuggled back into the warm comfort for one last moment before leaning on her elbow to look at her sleeping husband, then slipped out of bed.

Sophie's chest felt tight, it was difficult to breathe, '*I'll turn on the coffee, maybe have a cup before my shower.*' Wrapped in a soft robe she slipped her feet into fluffy mules and made her way to the kitchen. Waiting for the coffee to drip into her cup, she pondered the long perplexing night, the vivid world, so real, so intense. She sipped her coffee as she leaned on the counter in her small bright kitchen unable to shake the past few hours from her mind.

Sophie's emotions were tangled. Through the window, she waited for the sun to slip in over the fence and cover her gardens. She poured another cup of coffee and made toast for breakfast hoping to pull herself back into a normal mind set.

The usual rush of the morning to meet the trials of the day would not wait long. Sophie lingered at the window as her cup of coffee grew cold. The castle and the people felt as real as the counter she now leaned on. And Abba the king? He felt more real than the rest.

Wrapping her hands around a fresh cup of coffee, she breathed deep and let her feelings run free in all directions. She knew it was time to wake her husband and to take her shower and dress. They both held jobs that needed their attention. Yes, she would get back to her normal routine, the restless night with all it contained would have to wait. Closing her eyes Sophie felt tears pool. Why? The whole of it, her long night, the people and places were still so real. But why weep? What did all of it mean, if anything?

The images and the people were so real! In fact, Sophie knew they were real because they were people in her life here and now. Sophie shook her head hoping to clear out some of the useless clutter. She almost laughed. Most of the people Sophie spent the night with were very dear friends.

As she dressed for the day her husband came out of the shower wrapped in a towel, "Hello husband, time to go out into the world. The sun is shining so it should be a nice day."

"Must you always be so cheerful in the mornings?" Slipping long legs into jeans, continuing to dress, he knew she was already out of hearing.

Sophie returned to her toast and coffee and stood again at the kitchen window, looking out at her real world but with pictures of a different world flowing across her mind. What did it mean? She felt again the joy, the peace, the pain, the love between friends. And the love from and for Abba. She could still smell the rare fragrance hanging in the air. She chuckled thinking her friends, those so dear to her, were with her on her long sojourn through the night.

Sophie's husband came into the kitchen and poured coffee while watching his wife closely, "What's wrong?"

Sophie turned to look at her husband, "Oh Henri, you are spooky. What makes you think something is wrong?"

"Hey, I am the husband who loves everything about his wife and can certainly tell when her brow is creased in a certain way. Alerting me that something is not right. Got a heavy heart? Can I help?"

Sophie stepped to embrace the man she loved as he bent to kiss the top of her head. She said, "We'll talk later. I need to sort out things before I dump my chaos on you. It will have to wait."

"Are you sure it will wait?"

Looking up into his beautiful plain face she smiled, "It will wait until tonight, O.K.? I will always tell you right away if anything is seriously wrong."

Putting jam on a piece of toast, Henri ate his breakfast then reached for his briefcase. "Time to get this day underway."

When Henri left the room, Sophie remained at the table holding her empty cup. She finally stood and turned to pick up her coat and a folder she brought home from work last night.

Closing her eyes, she pictured her friends again as they were in her vision and then seeing them as she last saw them here in her present world just a few days ago.

This morning Monika would be out and about with a list of things to accomplish before the finish of her day. She would do her ombudsman check of a local care center, then help deliver meals-on-wheels to those unable to get out of their homes. Perhaps have a late lunch with friends. Financially independent, Monika gave in so many ways to those who could not defend for themselves. Priceless!

Sophie knew Bridget would be off to her work at a local primary school. And after dinner, she would volunteer to help make quilts for Veterans. She loved gathering blankets in the fall for the homeless shelter.

And Max? Max still charmed the ladies with his winks and tousled head of hair while still struggling not to fall off the fence into a dark ruined world. He mostly stayed safe, and Henri stayed extra close to help him through wobbly times.

Sophie, speaking aloud to no one said, "Yes, Henri would be there for his friend. Max would be safe as long as he remained close to the Father and to Henri."

Sophie's thoughts shifted to Darla, sweet gentle Darla. Darla would be up at three in the morning, running her small bakery, keeping her brother, Benjamin so busy he had little time left to think. His path had angled into the darkness years ago when he was too young to recognize the enemy and so many dangers out in the world. Darla carried the burden of the loss of her brother during those dark months pressing in with much prayer.

And now they were working, laughing, building new lives around their small business. Sophie knew the two were happy, wrapped in affection by many friends. They were winners against all odds. The thought brought a smile to Sophie, her eyes ready to spill over. Sophie shook herself and tied a scarf around her neck. Ah, dear people all. And the best of friends.

And there was Mary Elizabeth, dear Mary. Today as on all other days, she would be praying and encouraging others, spreading hope and her special kind of peace.

Sophie took a last look at her daily checklist and realized it was time to go. Her office at the non-profit was only a short drive from home.

Henri poked his head into the hall, "I started to leave and forgot something." She loved the twinkle in the eyes of that solemn face,

"What?"

"My kiss at the door. It keeps me warm no matter what."

They reached the front door together, Sophie stood on tiptoe to kiss him goodbye. Henri looked down at her, "Have fun out there today saving the world."

They both loved these last few moments before leaving, "Likewise to you, wonderful youth pastor that you are. Go forth and save a few young souls."

Sophie kissed him again soundly and turned toward her car,

"I'll be anxious to see you later."

"I truly hope so!" a sparkle in his eyes and raised brows betrayed his solemn expression.

"No really, I need you to help me understand my strange night of wonder during another time in another place. A dream, I suppose."

Sophie left him with his puzzled expression, "It will keep until tonight."

The day followed smoothly at work. Between appointments Sophie let pieces of her long night float up, trying to understand what it meant if anything. Perhaps it was just a dream! But it felt so real, so vivid, and the king, Abba? A name she knew well, she felt confident of that. *Lord, what are you trying to tell me? Open my ears to hear your voice.*

Working through the day with people and court filings, she would take a moment now and again to ponder the images still lingering. As the day's work finished in the late afternoon, Sophie bowed her head to pray, "You are my King, Abba, my healer, my provider."

Sophie lifted her head, "You are the Alpha and Omega, the First and the Last, the Beginning and the End." The scripture ran through her mind, "You are Who is and Who was and Who is to come, The Almighty." (Revelation 1:8)

Clearing her desk before leaning back in her chair, Sophie heard footsteps in the hall near her office. Tomorrow's work will keep.

"Time to go. It has been a long day. Are you about finished?" Mary Elizabeth stood in the doorway, keys in her hand. "There will be time tomorrow to heal more of this broken world."

Sophie looked up and smiled at the woman who found her, fed her, taught her, and loved her. Now partners in their small business, Sophie nodded, "Yes, Mary, it's time to go home." The scent of lavender hung in the air.

As she stood, Sophie looked at her dearest friend, "Are we rich yet?"

Mary Elizabeth in her calm way spoke and with a smile, said, Very!"

THE END